DATE DUE

PROMISE TO A
DEAD MAN

Other books by Kent Conwell:

PROMISE TO A DEAD MAN

•

Kent Conwell

AVALON BOOKS

NEW YORK

030706

F
Con

Published by Thomas Bouregy & Co., Inc.
160 Madison Avenue, New York, NY 10016

Library of Congress Cataloging-in-Publication Data

Conwell, Kent.
    Promise to a dead man / Kent Conwell.
        p. cm.
    ISBN 0-8034-9770-9 (hardcover : alk. paper)
    I. Title.

PS3553.O547P76 2006
813'.54—dc22

                              2005033848

PRINTED IN THE UNITED STATES OF AMERICA
ON ACID-FREE PAPER
BY HADDON CRAFTSMEN, BLOOMSBURG, PENNSYLVANIA

To my daughter, Susan. I love you.
And to my wife, Gayle.

Chapter One

W hen I rode into the small village, I had to look twice to make sure I was in Crockett, Texas instead of Roche, Texas. Seemed half of the businesses in the village were named after that Roche jasper.

The first building I spotted was Roche's Blacksmith, a shed twice as deep as it was wide. The stockade walls had been caulked with red mud and pine needles and topped off with a roof of rough split shingles.

Just north of the blacksmith was Roche's Livery, and directly across the wide street sat Roche's Saloon, a two-story clapboard building with balconies on three sides wearing a fresh coat of whitewash. A flight of stairs ran up the wall to the second floor. Next door was Roche's General Store. A few doors down the street was the milliner, next to the First Texas Bank, owner C. A. Roche. Across the street was the tonsorial parlor sitting next to the local jail.

With a wry grin, I shrugged. Looked like this Mister Roche would be getting some of my business for I planned to buy a cool beer, ask for directions, and then ride out. Three simple tasks that would take no longer than ten minutes, and within an hour or so, I would have put to rest a five-year-old promise to my dead friend and be on my way to California.

But that afternoon when I climbed down off my bay at the hitching rail in front of Roche's Saloon, I climbed down into trouble enough to change my life more than the federal prison in which I had spent the last few years of the War of Succession, what the Yankees called the War of the Rebellion and others, the Civil War.

Now, I'd grown accustomed to inhospitable towns for in making my way down to Crockett, Texas, from Fort Delaware—the federal prison in the middle of the Delaware River—I passed through many a small town and village, the inhabitants of which eyed drifters with suspicion, so the wary and guarded eyes that scrutinized my every move as I rode into Crockett were nothing new.

I couldn't blame them. The South was under reconstruction. At least, that's what the Yanks called it, "reconstruction," managed by Yankee carpetbaggers. The South labeled it outright thievery, but we had lost the war, and they had won. Nothing to do but live with it, a sobering fact I learned the hard way after I was captured back in '62 and sent to Fort Delaware as a prisoner of war.

So, I ignored the suspicious looks cast at me when I paused in front of the saloon to dust off my new boots I'd had specially made over in Nachitoche. Favoring my gimpy leg, I stomped across the worn boardwalk and entered the saloon.

Behind a fancy bar with a brass foot rail and a shiny top, a rotund bartender nodded and grinned. "Howdy, stranger. Welcome to Crockett."

I gestured to a sign leaning against the mirror behind the bar. "Howdy. How about one of those nickel beers?"

He drew a draft beer and slid it to me. "New in town, huh?"

"Just riding through." I slid a nickel across the bar and turned up the mug, downing several gulps at once. I shook my head in sheer pleasure at the refreshing swallows of cool beer after a long and dusty journey. "That's sure good. Wash the trail dust right out of a jasper's throat." I glanced in the mirror, noting that there were probably eight, nine hombres at poker tables, putting their games on hold while staring at me.

The bartender wiped at the shiny bar. "Come far?"

"Good piece." I took a sip this time then glanced over the saloon. "Nice place you have here."

He surveyed the saloon. "Reckon it is. Mister Roche, he always goes first class."

I downed the last of my beer and drew the back of my hand across my lips. "Only way to go if you can."

"Another one?"

"No, thanks, but I'd be obliged if you could give me directions to a ranch around here somewhere. The McCall spread."

The smile on his face froze. He cut his black eyes toward a table behind me. In the mirror, I saw two hombres push back from a table and saunter in my direction.

The one with his belly hanging over his gunbelt growled. "Why are you looking for the McCall's, Cowboy?"

Suppressing the urge to tell him it was none of his business, I fixed my eyes on him in the mirror, then slowly turned. I leaned back, resting my elbows on the bar, and faced the two. The first one leered at me with a crooked grin. The other rolled his shoulders and jutted a lantern-shaped jaw covered by several days of whiskers.

I'd never considered myself a bright jasper, but I was bright enough to see trouble brewing. With an affable grin, I replied, "Just business, Partner. Just passing through."

Lantern Jaw's eyes narrowed. "What kind of business?"

Behind me, the bartender spoke up. "Leave the cowboy alone, Cooter. He ain't causing no trouble."

Big Belly snapped. "Stay out of this, Frank. We know what we're doing."

Cooter bared his tobacco-stained teeth, revealing several gaps among them. "Well, you going to tell us or what?"

While I never looked for a fight, I never backed away from one either. I grew up with four brothers, and we were always fighting, which never proved a thing. "Look, Friend. What I'm doing here is my business, and only my business." I nodded to his table. "You'd be doing us both a favor by ambling back to your poker game."

Cooter grinned malevolently at his sidekick. "You hear what he said, Millikin? We'd be doing us a favor by going back to our poker game."

I grimaced. It appeared we were just about at the point of no return.

Millikin's crooked grin grew wider. "Yeah. I heard." He flexed his fingers. "You reckon he means it?"

The bartender broke in again. "Millikin, Cooter, stop it now. There ain't no sense in this."

The leer on Cooter's face grew wider. Ignoring the bartender, he growled. "I reckon you'll tell us, cowboy, or we'll just be forced to beat it out of you."

Remaining slouched back against the bar, I felt the empty beer mug pressing against my arm. I grinned.

Cooter frowned. "What are you grinning at?"

With a chuckle, I replied. "Every time I think I've

seen something so foolish that not even an idiot would do it, along comes an idiot who does it." I eased my elbow back, putting the handle of the beer mug within inches on my fingers.

Cooter frowned.

Millikin spoke up. "What do he mean by that, Cooter?"

Behind them, several guffaws came from the onlooking cowboys.

Cooter's face darkened. "I don't know, and I don't care. I'm going to clean up this place with you, Cowboy," he yelled, taking a step toward me and drawing back his right arm.

"Here," I said, grabbing the mug and lobbing it up in the air to him. "Catch."

"Huh? What?" Momentarily flustered, he stopped and grabbed clumsily for the mug.

That's when I stepped forward and busted him between the eyes, sending him sprawling backward across a poker table. I ducked as Millikin charged, swinging a roundhouse right that whipped over my head.

I jerked upright, at the same time throwing my arms up and sweeping him aside. I threw a right hook into his solar plexus, causing him to gasp for air, and followed with a left hook that spun him around. A twinge of pain shot through my gimpy right leg.

Behind me, Cooter roared like a bull. I spun around just in time to catch a massive fist on my chin. Stars exploded in my head, and my ears rang. I threw my arms up to protect my head and bulled into the wildly swinging man. I got directly up against him and drove punishing lefts and rights into a belly of iron, driving him back against the bar.

Suddenly, my head exploded, and I felt myself falling helplessly into a deep black hole.

Chapter Two

Somewhere in the back of my head a faint throbbing penetrated the darkness. Quickly it grew more and more painful, forcing me into consciousness. I became aware of the hard surface on which I lay. Slowly, I opened my eyes. I blinked several times, trying to focus them. Then I spotted the bars through which the morning sunlight shone.

After sorting the confusion raging in my head, I realized I was in jail.

With a long sigh, I closed my eyes. Jail. Just my luck. Like my old Pa had said, "Some have good luck, some bad. You was born with the bad, I reckon."

Slowly, I struggled to sit up. I glanced at my stockinged feet. That's when I realized my new boots were missing.

"Well, see you decided to come back to the living, cowboy."

I looked up at the deep voice into the face of the sheriff. He was an older jasper, thin as a rail, his rugged skin browned by the weather and a white mustache drooping down past his chin. Nodding, I managed to ask, "What am I doing here?"

With a laconic drawl he replied, "Disturbing the peace. Our town is a law-abiding one. I don't tolerate no trouble, not from the citizens and especially not from drifters."

Gingerly, I touched the sore spot on the back of my head. "You folks got a funny way of deciding who's disturbing who."

"I'm going on what I was told," he replied. "We don't cotton to strangers coming in and causing trouble."

Arching an eyebrow, I said. "That's what you were told, huh?"

He nodded and loosed a stream of tobacco into a brass cuspidor just outside the cell. "Yep."

I knew when I was licked. "Well, Sheriff, as soon as I can, I'll leave your little town. It's right unfriendly." I pointed to my feet. "What about my boots?"

"At the end of the bunk."

I reached for them, then stopped. "These aren't my boots," I said, holding up a pair of worn high-top boots with rundown heels.

He shrugged. "They was on the floor beside you when we picked you up." He sucked on a tooth for a moment, then grinned sheepishly. "Truth is, I was sort of curious as to why you took them off. I seen jaspers do strange things, but to take off your boots before you stir up trouble is mighty peculiar."

My head was throbbing too badly to argue. I pulled the boots on and managed to stand. "How do I get out of here, Sheriff?"

"Pay your fine," he drawled. "Ten dollars."

I reached for my wallet. Bad luck settled on my shoulders again. It was empty. Whoever had taken my boots had also taken my money, twenty-three dollars.

"Ain't got none? Five days if you can't pay the fine."

Shaking my head, I removed my vest. "I got it." I loosened a thread on my vest and pulled out a greenback. "Here you are." I could smell the coffee brewing on the potbellied stove. "You got an extra cup for an ex-prisoner, Sheriff."

He laughed. "Reckon so. Come on over and sit. Whereabouts you from, Cowboy?"

"Name's Nelson, Davy Nelson. Before the war, I come from Honey Grove up near the Red River." I pulled out a bag of Bull Durham. At least, whoever had taken my boots and money had left me my cigarette makings. I rolled one and offered it to the sheriff, and over a cup of six-shooter coffee and a cigarette, I filled him in on what I had set out to do.

Frowning, he said, "But the war was over two years

ago. It take you that long to get here from Delaware, wherever that place be?"

Laying my hand on my right leg, I explained. "A guard shot me by accident. Broke the bone. Truth is, I was lucky that I had a Yank doctor who refused to turn me out at the end of the war. I'd probably have died from the infection. No, sir, he kept me in the hospital for over a year, fighting the infection in this leg. Had to rebreak it once. It's taken me the rest of the time to get down here. So now, I'm about at the end of my promise to Russell McCall."

Grimacing, he shook his head. "I'd heard that Russ had been killed in the war. His family knew too, but they didn't know none of the if's and when's." He grinned at me. "Reckon you must've been mighty good friends for you to travel such a far piece."

I thought about Russell, and that crooked grin he always wore. "Reckon so. Reckon when you're sharing a hole with another jasper and bullets are flying all about, you tell each other things you'd never dream of telling another soul." I snubbed out my cigarette and rose. "Thanks, Sheriff. All I need now is to find the McCall place."

"Easy. Take the west road toward Centerville. About two hours out, you'll see their place. It's just before you get to the river.

"Thanks." I headed for the door. When I opened it, I spotted Roche's bank across the street. "By the way,

Sheriff," I said, looking back. "This Roche fellow. He own everything in town?"

Swain arched an eyebrow. "He wants to."

My stomach was gnawing on my backbone I was so hungry, but I was anxious to get shed of this town. My pony was still at the hitching rail. I needed to feed and water him before leaving, so I headed for the livery where I paid four bits for grain and water.

Leaving him at the livery, I ambled over to the general store for a few supplies. I figured on pulling up outside of town and whipping up a meal. I'd had enough of Crockett hospitality.

I waited at the counter while a clerk wearing a long white apron over his portly belly counted out change to a bone-thin jasper in a black suit that contrasted sharply with his pale face. "Here you are, Ezekiel. Two dollars and six bits. By the way, did Mister Roche get the top floor finished at the bank?"

The pasty-faced man snapped open a coin purse and carefully folded the bills into it. "Yesterday, Calvin. He plans to store bank records up there." He glanced at me, turned up his nose, and primly marched to the front door.

The clerk grinned at me. "That was Ezekiel Watts. Don't pay him no mind, stranger. He's a bookkeeper and notary over at the bank. Knows more about Mister Roche's business than Roche hisself does. Kinda stuck up at times. Now, what can I do for you?"

I gave him my order, which he quickly filled. "Thanks," I said, heading for the door. Just before I reached it, two waddies strode past, the two I'd fought with the day before, and the big one, Cooter, was wearing my new boots. I watched until they disappeared into the saloon, and then I set my goods on the counter. "I'll be back," I told the merchant. "I got me an errand to take care of."

I stopped outside the jail and read the name on the door, Sheriff Jess Swain. I hurried inside.

"I've got to have a witness, Sheriff. I know who stole my boots and money. I can prove it, but I don't want to get myself in any more trouble around here. I've had all the trouble I want in my life already."

"Proof, you say?"

"Yep. Hard proof."

Raising a skeptical eyebrow, he growled. "Such as?"

"One boot has my initials in it, and the other carries a knife. I had them made special over in Nachitoche."

His eyes grew suspicious. "Funny place to carry a knife."

We pushed through the batwing doors into the saloon. Cooter and Millikin were seated at a table with two other hombres playing poker. I strode across the room and glared down at Cooter.

He grinned up at me. "Back for more?" The others at the table snickered.

"You stole my boots and money. I want them back, now."

His eyes narrowed. He rose to his feet. "You're a liar." He stuck out his chin.

He expected me to respond. I did, but not the way he thought. Immediately, I slammed a straight right into his throat.

His eyes popped open wide, and he grabbed at his throat, gagging, trying to catch his breath. He stumbled back into his chair. I felt a pair of arms grab at me, but I ducked under them. At the same time, I shucked my Colt and, spinning on my heel, whipped the barrel of the handgun in a arc, slamming it into the face of the jasper behind me.

Millikin screamed and grabbed at his cheek. Blood surged through his fingers and dripped down on his chest. He staggered back a few steps, his eyes filling with fear.

Sheriff Swain stood motionless, his mouth gaping open. I holstered my six-gun and yanked a boot off Cooter. "Take a look, Sheriff. Inside the leg, DWN, David William Nelson." Then I yanked off the other boot. "And here's the knife, just like I said, Sheriff."

Swain nodded slowly. "Reckon you were right, Davy. Them is your boots." He hesitated, then with a grin continued. "How much money did you say you was missing?"

"Twenty-three dollars."

Cooter was still sitting, still gagging, still clutching

his throat. The sheriff reached under Cooter's arm and retrieved a wallet from the choking man's vest and counted out twenty-three dollars. "There you go, Mister Nelson. Now, I don't reckon there's nothing keeping you in Crockett, is there?"

With a broad grin, I replied. "No, sir, not one thing."

Chapter Three

The countryside around Crockett was hilly, covered with lush meadows of blue grama grasses with sideoat grasses mixed in, and dotted with stands of tall sentinel pines and mottes of oak and pecan.

The narrow trace on which I rode over the meadows curved in and around the stands of forests. The sun was directly overhead when I spotted a battered sign almost torn apart by gunfire. I read the sign: *Bar M. Ed McCall.*

Leaning forward, I patted my bay's neck and studied the narrow road disappearing into a stand of pine on the crest of a hill. "Well, fella, here it is. What we've been trying to reach for the last nine months. Do our job here, and it's on to California and a brand-new life." With a click of my tongue and gentle pressure from my knees, I sent the bay up the hill in a trot.

Suddenly, a shot rang out and the ground off to my left exploded, sending clods of hard dirt in every direction. My pony shied. "Whoa, boy. Whoa," I muttered, pulling him back under control.

"Hold up right there, Mister," a voice called from the pines on the crest of the slope. "Don't take another step."

That was one thing he didn't have to tell me. I'd already pulled up. I sat motionless in the saddle, staring at the pines from where the shot had come.

The voice called out again. "You're on private property, Cowboy. Main road's yonder behind you."

I shouted back. "This the McCall spread?"

There was a moment of hesitation. "Might be."

"I come to see Ed McCall."

Another pause. "He's dead."

"It's about Russell, his boy."

Several seconds passed with no response, and then a cautious voice called out. "Come on up, but come slow."

As I drew near the pines, a needle thin jasper with a wad of tobacco in his cheek stepped from behind a tree and held the muzzle of his Henry repeater on me. An older hombre, his narrow face was hard, and his cold eyes studied me warily. He shifted the wad of tobacco to his other cheek and loosed a stream of juice on the ground. "What about Russell?"

I bit my tongue. I was growing mighty tired of every hombre in this part of the state asking me questions that were none of his business. In an even voice, I replied, "You part of the family?"

"I work here."

Then I knew who he was. "I don't reckon you're the one named Speck."

A look of surprise filled his eyes. Then his brows knit in a frown. "Who are you? How'd you know my name?"

Relaxing, I slumped back in my saddle. "I was in the war with Russell. He told me all about this place here. He even told me about the time you pulled him out of the river when he got caught in a flood."

Speck's face softened, and a grin spread over his lips. He lowered the Henry. "Yep. I never could get much work done around here for keeping that young feller out of trouble." He stepped forward and offered me his hand. "Name's Speck Webster."

"Davy Nelson," I replied, taking his firm grasp. "Pleased to meet you, Speck."

"Come on, Davy," he said, walking ahead of me up the trail. "My pony's up yonder a piece." He glanced back at me. "We heard that Russell was killed in the war."

"That's why I'm here. I was with him when he died."

Speck paused before climbing on his horse and looked at me. His face grew somber. "Reckon the family will be mighty pleased to see you."

At the crest of the hill, I spotted the ranch buildings sprawled on the top of a smaller hill about half a mile in the distance. I had to admire Ed McCall's choice of location. The buildings were surrounded by thick stands of pine on two sides and steep hills on a third. To the west, the ground dropped steeply to the flood plain of the Trinity River that Russell had talked about.

Everywhere I looked I saw cattle grazing, which I thought unusual. Most spreads don't graze the whole range. Instead, they loose herd the cattle in a particular section, giving the remainder of the range a chance to revitalize itself with fresh growth and essential nutrients.

At even a casual glance, it was obvious that this ranch, which, according to Russell had once been a top-notch spread, was now slowly rusting away.

My hunch was verified when we rode past the barn. Two jaspers looked up from mending tack, a job that could be handled at night, not during the day when wranglers needed to be out with the cattle.

To my surprise, I felt a surge of anger toward the two. If Russell were here, I told myself, those two jaspers would be working their tails off. All I could do was shake my head. Sorry, Russell, I said to myself.

* * *

A young woman in jeans and a plaid shirt stepped out on the porch as we rode up. Kate! Had to be. Like Russell had said, she had the biggest brown eyes I'd ever seen. By now, she must be in her early twenties, but Russell had never told me just how pretty she was. She wore her black hair short. Her face was tanned, and across her forehead was a line of white skin where her hat had protected her from the sun.

She nodded in my direction. "Who do you have there, Speck?"

Speck reined up. His voice quivered slightly. "Miss Kate. This here's Davy Nelson." He paused, and in choked voice added. "He's come to tell us about Russell."

She looked up at me, momentarily bewildered.

"I was with him when he died," I explained. "I promised him I'd tell his family about it."

She stared at me, shocked by the sudden under-standing of my words, then quickly gathered herself. "Call the men, Speck. Tell them to come to the parlor." I could see the pain in her eyes when she smiled sadly up at me. "I'd be pleased if you'd come inside, Mister Nelson. I'd like for you to meet my mother."

The main house had been constructed with heavy beams, hand-hewn from the tall pines around the ranch and then squared to fit. Great timbers spanned from wall to wall, and above, hand-split shingles formed the roof.

Her hair solid white, Mrs. McCall sat in a rocking chair, slowly rocking, staring straight ahead into the dancing flames of the stone fireplace. "Mother, this is Mister Nelson. He's come to tell us about Russell."

The elderly woman gave no indication she had heard her daughter's words. I nodded. "Pleased to meet you, Mrs. McCall."

No response. Just rocking, back and forth, back and forth.

Keeping her eyes on her mother, Miss Kate explained. "Mother's been like that since Pa was killed. She took word of Russ's death hard, and then when Pa was found out on the road, she—well, she's not been the same since."

I didn't know exactly what to say except, "I'm sorry."

At that moment, two young boys raced in, pushing and shoving each other. "Boys," Kate snapped. "Behave yourselves. We have company."

The two youths looked at me curiously. "This one," she said, indicating the younger one with blond hair and freckles, "his name's Samuel Allen McCall. We call him Sam, and this one is Raymond James. He goes by Ray." The older young man was dark complexioned like his sister.

At that moment, Speck came in followed by a gimpy legged old man whom I instantly knew had to be the cook, Smoke, and the two hombres I'd spotted out in the barn mending tack.

"You know Speck." She nodded to the shorter of the two wranglers. "This is Otsie Bets and this is John Bratton," she said, gesturing to the taller of the two. Both men wore surly grimaces. "And this is Smoke, our cook."

The old man nodded to me. From the way his chin seemed much too close to his nose, I knew he had no teeth, and was probably too cantankerous to wear his false ones, if he even had any.

Kate turned back to Speck. "Where's Red?"

Smoke replied, "Out on the south range, Miss Kate."

A tiny frown wrinkled her forehead. "I wish he was here. Oh, well, we'll tell him later." She drew a deep breath. "Mister Nelson was with Russ when he died. He promised Russ he'd tell us—" she hesitated, "—about the war, about what happened." She looked at me hopefully. "Please, Mister Nelson. Have a seat." She gestured to a stuffed wingback chair.

Awkwardly, I sat, holding my battered Stetson on my lap and my bad leg out straight. "Sorry about the leg, ma'am. It doesn't bend so easy anymore."

She glanced at it, then jerked her gaze back to my face. "The war?"

I nodded.

With the exception of the two wranglers, they were all staring at me expectantly. I cleared my throat and in a soft voice, began. "I met Russell when we both joined the Fourth Texas Cavalry up in Fort Worth in

June of '61. We ended up in the same tent. We hit it off right away." I glanced at Mrs. McCall, but she just continued rocking, staring straight ahead.

"The Fourth was ordered east where we fought at Bloody Ridge then on to places like Hampton Roads and Blue Creek and Boone's Court House in Virginia." I paused as the memories rushed back, bringing with them the anguish and fear with which we all lived during those harrowing days.

I must have fallen silent for several moments, for Kate's concerned voice cut into my thoughts. "Are you all right, Mister Nelson? Would you like a drink of water?"

"Huh?" I looked around in surprise, then realized where I was. "No. No, I'm fine. Anyway, after Virginia we were transferred to Garland's Brigade under General D. H. Hill. That was in April. By then, Russell had been wounded once."

Kate gasped, but I quickly explained. "Just a graze. Took off some of the skin. Anyway, in May, we attacked Fair Oaks near Seven Pines in Virginia." Shaking my head, I continued my story, my voice growing softer, my eyes gazing into the past. "It was pure butchery. I heard later that over five thousand Union soldiers were killed or wounded or just plain missing. And over six thousand Confederates."

Speck muttered a soft curse.

"Our ponies were shot out from under us. Russ rode a big black stallion. It fell on him. Crushed him something terrible." I left out how the blood ran from his mouth; how when he coughed, his blood had sprayed my face; how he had cried tears from the pain of his crushed ribs; how he had begged me all night to make the pain go away; or how his dying groan still sent chills down my spine. I stared at the floor, those horrifying memories filling my head. Woodenly, I continued. "I pulled him into a clump of bushes and stayed with him all night. Next morning, he squeezed my hand and made me promise to come and tell you what happened." I paused and swallowed at the lump in my throat brought back by those dark memories. "He—he said to tell you all he loved you. And then he closed his eyes." For several moments, I remained silent, staring into the past, lost in my memories. Softly, I added. "I was about halfway finished burying Russell when the Yanks captured me." I pressed my lips together and stared at the heavy beams overhead. "The two who caught me let me finish burying him."

After a moment, I jerked myself back to the present.

Mrs. McCall continued rocking, staring into space. Tears rolled down Kate's cheeks. Sam and Ray, her younger brothers, stared at me in stunned disbelief. Speck wiped a tear off his weathered and wrinkled cheek, and old Smoke just shook his head. I couldn't read the expressions on the faces of Bratton or Bets.

Kate cleared her throat. "Did—did he suffer much?"

"No, ma'am. He was mostly unconscious until the

very end." That was a lie, but I didn't reckon the good Lord would hold it against me.

There had been enough pain spread around the country. No sense in dishing out any more.

Chapter Four

I had figured on telling my story and then riding on out for California. From stories I'd heard, the state sounded like a golden land, and it was as far away from the battlefields of the war as I could get.

But, for some reason, I didn't argue too hard when Kate asked me to stay for supper and spend the night in the bunkhouse. "At least when you leave in the morning, you'll have a full belly and a good night's sleep behind you."

Red Tucker showed up for supper. He was an amiable redhead full of wild stories that he kept telling while we put ourselves around platters of fried steak, bowls of succotash, hot sourdough biscuits, and red-eye gravy.

Bratton and Bets stayed to themselves, every once in a while giving me cold looks.

I was squatting against the hitching rail outside the chuck house later, smoking a cigarette, when Speck ambled out. He squatted beside me. "Mighty white of you to do that for the family, Davy."

"Russell would have done it for me."

Neither of us spoke for a few moments.

I cleared my throat. "What's into Bets and Bratton? They're about as friendly as a stomped-on rattler."

He chuckled. "That's them. I been after Miss Kate to turn them loose. They ain't much help."

"Why don't she?"

He grunted. "Around here, help's hard to get. Especially for us."

Before I could respond, young Sam came skidding up. Breathlessly, he peppered me with questions. "Mister Nelson, tell me about the war. What was it like? Were you ever wounded? How many Yanks did you kill?"

His questions would probably have kept coming had Miss Kate not walked up. She wore a fresh change of clothes. "Sam. Stop badgering Mister Nelson, you hear?"

Speck pushed to his feet and laid his hand on the young boy's shoulder. "Your sis is right, boy. Come on out to the barn and help me take care of my pony."

Stubbing out my cigarette, I rose to my feet and we watched as the two strode across the hardpan to the barn.

"I want to thank you again, Mister Nelson."

"Davy, ma'am. I get uncomfortable when someone calls me Mister."

She laughed, a tinkling little sound. "All right. Davy it is. I'm Kate. Not Miss Kate, just Kate."

I nodded and grinned. "Done."

For several moments, neither of us spoke. It was nice just being close to her. She had a clean, fresh smell about her.

Finally, Kate broke the silence. "I was relieved to hear about Russ. I always knew he wasn't coming back, but until you know for certain, you always wonder." She looked up at me as if asking my opinion.

"Human nature, I reckon."

"I suppose." She drew a deep breath and released it slowly. "I guess I always held out hope that someday he would return and help run the ranch." She shook her head slowly.

"Running a spread like this is a big job."

She laughed again. "Tell me something I don't know."

Another few minutes of silence passed. She pointed to a nearby hill lit by the stars. "Up there is the family cemetery. Pa's there, and three brothers. It hurts that Russ won't be there, but we'll put up a headstone anyway."

"Reckon Russell would like that."

She looked up at me. "Where you heading when you leave here?"

"I kinda got me a hankering to see California."

"Is that where you're from?"

"No, Ma'am. I'm from Honey Grove, Texas. That's back north, up near the Red River. That's where I grew up. My folks are buried there."

"Any other family?"

"Had some older brothers, but the war took them." I shook my head. "One thing's for certain, I wouldn't care to head back to Crockett. That's a mighty unfriendly town."

When she looked up, the moonlight illumined the knowing grin on her face. "Don't tell me. You had a run-in with Carl Roche or some of his men." She laughed when she saw the surprise on my face. "Not many folks come away from there with good feelings about the town. That's one of our problems out here."

I leaned back against the hitching rail and crossed my arms over my chest. "I don't understand."

Her voice grew sharp and bitter. "Carl Roche is a Yankee carpetbagger who by now just about owns all of Crockett."

"From the signs I saw with his name everywhere, I figured he owned a heap."

"And he wants our place. He owns the bank that carries our mortgage. As long as Pa was alive, we did fine, but now—" her voice drifted off.

"Now what?" I was mildly curious about Carl Roche.

Even in the pale starlight, I could see the anger knitting her eyebrows. "He owns the general store. His men always hurrah the boys when they go in to pick up supplies. And according to Speck and Red, every so often, some of our cattle go missing. We've never caught anyone, and I can't prove it, but I believe Carl Roche is behind it all, even the death of my father."

I pushed away from the hitching rail. "What makes you say that?"

Kate stared in the direction of the cemetery. "We found Pa out on the road, shot in the back. He had gone into town to make the yearly mortgage payment. Roche claims Pa never made the payment. Come this January, we'll owe two years. If we don't pay it, Roche will foreclose."

"What happened to the money he was going to pay the mortgage with?"

Skepticism evident in her words, Kate looked around at me. "They say he gambled it away in Roche's saloon." She shook her head adamantly. "But that's a lie. Pa never gambled. Claimed he was too unlucky."

"What did the sheriff have to say about it all?"

"Oh, Jess Swain is a good man, but he couldn't find anything to prove otherwise."

I shook my head slowly. "Any chance of making this year's payment?"

"No," she replied, her voice forlorn. "Not a chance."

We lapsed into silence.

After a few moments, she sighed and looked up. "I

apologize for spilling all my problems to you. I appreciate you taking time to tell us about Russ. If I don't see you before you leave in the morning, take care."

"You too," I replied.

With one last smile, she turned and headed for the main house. I watched until she closed the door behind her and a yellow glow lit the window shades in a side bedroom.

Absently, I lit another cigarette, studying the main house and pondering how unfair life can be when unprincipled men achieve power.

Maybe someone should do something about it.

On the other hand, last time I set out back in '61 to rectify what I considered an inequitable situation, I lost six years out of my life.

I didn't want to lose another six.

Chapter Five

The last time I had a good night's sleep was before the war, and that night in the McCall bunkhouse was no exception. I lay awake, staring at the darkness above me, thinking about Russell and Kate; about the ranch; and about Carl Roche.

I didn't want to think about them. I truly wanted to get on with my life, which I figured meant that I should get on to California, find myself a job, and start building a future. I didn't need or want any of the problems Kate and her family had. Still, I couldn't put Russell McCall out of my mind.

He and I had fought and bled side by side. The adversity we faced together had created a kinship—we became like brothers. I tried to push him from my mind, but the terrifying days and nights that we helped each other live through refused to go away.

After midnight, I rolled out of my bunk and slipped outside for a cigarette. Pain shot up my leg, worsening my already pronounced limp. I stared up at the Big Dipper in the sky, which was clear as spring water, trying unsuccessfully to sort my thoughts. Finally, I shook my head in frustration. "Nope," I muttered. "I'm not sticking around. I'm riding out right after breakfast." I flipped my cigarette onto the hardpan and limped inside, trying to ignore the guilt nagging at me.

I awakened next morning with the lantern light from the chuck house shining through the window and falling across my bunk. I climbed out from under the blankets and quickly dressed, planning on grabbing a cup of coffee and maybe a couple hot biscuits and riding out. I wouldn't admit it, but I didn't feel like facing the other wranglers.

Outside the chuck house was a stack of firewood, so I gathered an armload and hauled it inside.

Smoke looked around when I stomped in. A broad grin spread over his craggy face when he spotted the firewood. "Much obliged, Mister Nelson. Mighty thoughtful of you."

"My pleasure. After that dandy supper last night, I figured this is the least I could do."

He gestured to the sawbuck table. "Sit. Coffee's

brewing. I'm putting biscuits on now," he said, plopping a covered black pot down on the stove with a resounding clang.

I rested my elbows on the table and leaned forward. "Big spread you folks have here."

The old cook slapped slabs of venison in the skillet. "Yep. The Bar M used to be a fine one when Ed McCall was around. Kinda gone to seed now. Miss Kate, she does her best, but she's got a heart of gold." He continued talking as he turned the frying venison. "Sometimes you got to be hard. Old Ed, he knew when to be hard and when to go easy. Russ was like that too."

He frowned, and his lips quivered slightly as an expression of sadness flickered momentarily over his face. He shook his head and turned to me. "I'm too old to worry about sticking my nose in someone else's business, so I'm just going to out and say it. What are the chances of you hanging around here and helping us get this spread back to where it once was?"

At that moment, the coffee boiled over. Smoke muttered a curse and quickly slid the pot off the stove. With his back to me, he continued. "Way I see it, it took a heap of gumption and determination for you to come all this way to tell us about Russ. You could've just kept on riding. We need that kind of gumption around here."

The guilt I'd felt the night before flooded back.

Like a little banty rooster, he turned and stared at

me, one hand holding a fork, the other a dishcloth. "Well?"

Part of me wanted to say yes, but another part remembered the six years I had been away doing another's job.

"It ain't going to be easy, Mister Nelson. Cattle is being stolen; the two boys need a firm hand; half of the ranch hands are worthless; and the carpetbagger banker is trying to get his greedy hands on the Bar M." He hesitated, then added, "I reckon if Russ was here he could handle it all, but he ain't here, and he ain't never going to be here." He paused and drew a deep breath. "And Miss Kate, she tries mighty hard, but she can't do it on her own."

He clamped his lips shut, but what he had left unsaid was as clear as the Big Dipper had been the night before. I cleared my throat. "So that leaves me. Is that what you're saying?"

He pondered my question a moment, then nodded emphatically. "Yes, sir. I reckon that is exactly what I'm saying."

At that moment, the other hands tromped in and took their places. Joe Bratton paused before taking a seat and sneered at me. "See you're trying to get an early start, huh? Smart man who knows when to leave."

Otsie Bets snickered.

I frowned, wondering just what had prompted his remark.

Speck snapped at Bratton. "Sit down and eat, Bratton. You got a heap of work ahead of you today."

The sneer on Bratton's face grew wider. He snorted and plopped his big carcass down at the table. "Whatever you say, boss."

The sneering cowpoke's remarks rankled me, but I held my temper. Within an hour, I'd be on the trail. All of this would be behind me. Smoke plopped the coffee on the table. "Drink 'er down, boys. It's strong enough to do the work of ten men."

Throughout breakfast, I could feel Smoke's eyes on me, but I deliberately ignored him. Even as I left the chuck house that morning, I knew he was still watching me.

A few minutes later, I paused at the hitching rail at the main house and surveyed the ranch once again. It was just like Russell had described. Spreading oaks shaded the spring-fed swimming hole at the base of the hill. The overflow of water formed a tiny stream that meandered across the broad flood plain to the river beyond. I tried to imagine the ranch in its prime.

Yes, sir. In my mind's eye, I could see it in the spring, the range lush and green with thick grasses, the water cool and sweet, the cattle fat and content.

A soft voice jerked me back to the present. "Good morning." I looked around. Kate stood on the porch. "Looks like you're ready to leave," she said.

I thought I sensed a trace of disappointment in her

voice. "Yep. Just wanted to tell you thanks for the bunk and grub."

Tiny wrinkles etched her forehead. "Our thanks to you, Davy, for bringing us word of Russ. We'll always be grateful."

"The least I could do, Kate. I owed Russell."

She smiled sadly.

For a few awkward moments, we looked at each other. Nodding one last time, I touched my finger to the brim of my Stetson and rode away.

I paused at the top of the hill and looked back, suddenly filled with a strange and puzzling emptiness.

Back to the west, I spotted Speck pushing a few head of cattle south. He saw me and raised an arm in recognition. I waved back. The feeling that I was making a terrible mistake by riding away filled the emptiness in my chest.

"Besides," I muttered to my horse. "I've been gone six years. No one is waiting for you or me anywhere. What's another few months going to hurt?"

So, instead of turning west, I headed back to Crockett. For what I had in mind, I had to see Sheriff Swain.

Chapter Six

Sheriff Swain looked up in surprise when I pushed through the door. "Well, I didn't expect to see you around here, Mister Nelson. Figured you'd taken care of business with the McCalls and done rode on out."

I stood hipshot in front of his desk, favoring my gimpy leg. "The McCalls are my business, Sheriff. That's what I wanted to talk to you about."

A puzzled frown wrinkled his rugged forehead. "I don't follow you."

Tipping my hat to the back of my head, I explained. "I figure on working for the Bar M. I've been told that they've run into problems when they come to town, especially when they pick up supplies over at Roche's General Store. I hope there won't be any trouble when we come in."

Sheriff Swain pursed his lips thoughtfully, then leaned back in his chair. "Let me make one thing clear, Mister Nelson. This here's a peaceable town. I keep it that way. Now, I know Mister Roche wants the Bar M. That's another matter. Nothing I can do about it as long as he stays legal, but there won't be no trouble in my town when anyone picks up supplies or anything else. I won't have it."

I studied him closely as he spoke. He came across as an honest man who was determined to do exactly what he said. "I don't want any trouble either, Sheriff. I've just come back from over six years of trouble among some mighty inhospitable hombres. I just want to be left alone, but if anyone comes snapping at me, I'll snap right back." I eyed him steadily.

A wry grin ticked up one side of his thin lips. "I believe that, Mister Nelson. I saw what you did to Cooter and Millikin yesterday. Yes, sir, I can believe that."

As I rode past Roche's Saloon on the way out of town, Cooter Fain and George Millikin stepped out through the batwing doors. They jerked to a halt on the boardwalk and glared at me. Millikin sported a bandage on his right cheek. I touched my finger to the brim of my hat and dipped my head to them.

Back at the ranch, Kate came out of the barn as I rode in, a puzzled frown on her face. I rode over to meet her. "What happened? You forget something?"

"Yep. Reckon I did, Kate. I reckon I forgot to ask you if you needed another hand around this place."

She stared at me in disbelief. A faint smile flickered on her lips. "What did you say?"

I made a sweeping gesture with my arm. "I'd like to come to work here. How about it?"

She laughed uncertainly. "Well, yes—but—I can't afford you."

"Don't worry about that." I shook my head. "Food and keep is good enough."

"What about California?"

With a shrug, I said, "It's been there a mighty long time. I reckon it can wait a few months longer." I paused, then added, "I figure Russell will rest easier if I was to give you a hand in bailing this place out of its problems, if you can use me."

"Can I use you? Of course I can use you. I've been trying to run this place by myself for the last year since Pa was killed. You can take over as foreman."

"Foreman? What about Speck? Won't that rankle him?"

"Speck?" She frowned and then shook her head. "He isn't the foreman. I am. I tell him what to do, and he tells the men for me."

"In that case, I'd be right glad to take over, but I have to warn you, I expect hard work from every cow-puncher from can't see to can't see. I reckon you'll have some gripes, but I learned a long time back that if you want to get to the top of the hill, you got to do a heap of climbing."

That night before supper in the chuck house, Kate made the announcement. For the most part, everyone seemed content with her decision except Bets and Bratton. Bratton twisted his lips into a snarl and whispered into Bets' ear.

I knew right then that there was going to be a showdown with Joe Bratton eventually.

I wasn't wrong. No sooner had I limped into the bunkhouse than Bratton, who was seated on his bunk, snarled. "Look here, boys. We got us a new foreman who knows how to sweet-talk the boss."

Otsie Bets laughed.

Speck stood up. "Hold on, Bratton. That's—"

"Step away, Speck," I said softly, interrupting him. "If Bratton's got something on his chest, let him get it off, because when he's finished, I plan to air out a few gripes of my own."

Bratton rose slowly to his feet and rolled his shoulders. "Yeah, I got a gripe. I got me a big gripe. I don't cotton to no gimpy greenhorn coming in here and figuring he's going to tell me what to do." He jabbed his meaty finger at his own chest. "I been here three years and I know my job," he said, stabbing his finger at me this time. "So don't you reckon on telling me nothing."

My voice grew cold and hard. "Now listen to me,

Bratton. I'm foreman here. You'll either do what I say or draw your pay. It's that simple."

He narrowed his eyes. "Says who?" He flexed his fingers into knotty fists. "You?"

I kept my eyes fixed on his. "If that's what it takes."

He guffawed. "There ain't no rail-thin cripple around that can make me do something if I don't figure on it."

For someone who had wanted to steer away from trouble, I had managed to find myself neck deep in it. I sighed in resignation. "How do you want it, Bratton? Fists or six-guns?"

He figured I'd start crawfishing, so my blunt question took him by surprise. For a moment, his belligerence eased. "I ain't no gunnie."

I dropped my own gunbelt. "Fine with me. Outside. I don't favor tearing this place up just to teach you a lesson."

Speck and Red snickered. Bratton's face twisted in anger.

Just as I threw open the door, Speck yelled. "Davy, look out."

In the next second, a fist slammed into the back of my head, sending me stumbling through the door and flipping over the hitching rail just outside. I landed on my back on the hardpan.

With a shout of triumph, Bratton charged me, planning on stomping me to a grease spot. When he raised his boot above me, I slammed my boot heel into his other leg, knocking him off balance. I rolled to my feet and faced him.

We were about the same height, but he had me by fifty pounds. I figured his head was like granite, but remembering the enormous meal he had put away at supper, I decided to go for his belly.

"All right, Gimp. I'm going to tear your head off." He growled and charged at me, grunting as he swung lefts and rights wildly. I stepped under his roundhouses and slammed a right hook deep into his stomach.

He grunted and stumbled back, surprised. I lowered my head and waded into him, following up my hook with three uppercuts into his belly and a couple hooks into his kidneys.

With a savage grunt, he wrapped his arms about me and lifted me off my feet, squeezing my ribs. Then he hurled me to the ground. Stars exploded in my head, but instinctively I rolled aside just as a boot slammed to the hardpan beside my head.

I kicked my left leg forward, catching him behind the knees and whipping his feet from under him. He landed on his back with a jolt, and as he rolled toward me, I kicked him between the eyes with the heel of my boot.

Quickly climbing to my feet, I taunted the large man. "Come on, Bratton. Get up. You're not going to let a cripple get the best of you, are you?"

With a roar, he jumped to his feet and, head down, charged toward me again. At the last second, I stepped aside and buried my fist in his belly up to my wrist. He grunted and spun around, grabbing me about the chest. With an animal growl, he jerked me off the ground, planning on throwing me onto the hardpan once again.

Before he could move, I slammed my forehead into his nose and shattered it. Screaming in pain, he dropped me and grabbed at his nose. Blood gushed through his fingers onto his chest. Swinging left and right hooks, I was all over him like mud on a hog.

Bratton stood helpless, holding his nose and crying. After half a dozen unanswered punches, I backed away and glared at him. Gasping for breath, I said, "You got any more complaints, Bratton?"

He didn't reply. I figured that meant he didn't have any further complaining to do.

Looking around at the other cowpunchers, I nodded to the bunkhouse. "All right, boys. Let's hit the bedrolls. I'll give out tomorrow's assignments at breakfast."

That night, I lay on my side with my .44 Colt in my hand, watching Bratton's bunk. I didn't go to sleep until much later after seeing the hulking man's bulky shadow tiptoe out of the bunkhouse and moments later, hearing the clatter of hooves as he rode away.

Chapter Seven

There was a conspicuous vacancy at the breakfast table next morning. Otsie Bets was subdued, muttering vague responses to questions about Joe Bratton's disappearance.

Speck looked up from his plate of flapjacks the size of saddle blankets and winked at me. "You're sporting a purty little bruise on your cheek this morning, Davy."

I shrugged off the remark. Joe Bratton was gone, and as far as I was concerned, forgotten. "Where's the best graze on the range around here, Speck?"

Red answered for him. "Southeast a mile or so."

At that moment, Smoke returned from taking breakfast up to the main house. "Miss Kate says to tell you she'll be ready soon as she has her breakfast."

"Good." I turned back to the men. "All right. I want you boys to gather the cows and push them over to the southeast range. Loose herd them. We'll keep them there for a spell. Growing season's about over but I want to give the rest of the range a change to breathe some. Maybe pick up a few inches of growth before winter."

Red nodded. "You bet." He and Speck exchanged big grins.

I continued. "I'm going into town today to pick up supplies. Kate's driving the buckboard."

As we spoke, Otsie Bets' eyes shifted from one to the other like a frightened weasel.

"Could be trouble, Davy," Speck said. "Roche owns the store. He's been giving us a hard time the last few trips we've made."

"So I've heard. Just what does he do?" I sipped my coffee.

Smoke spoke up. "It ain't him. It's them saddle tramps what work for him. They do their best to stir up whatever trouble they can."

Red arched an eyebrow. "They act like they're just hurrahing us, but they're really trying to egg us into a gunfight."

Outside, the sun was peeking over the horizon, painting the eastern sky with a golden orange. I climbed away from the sawbuck table and snugged my hat down. "Get a move on, boys. Let's get to work. I'll hook up the rig."

Kate was standing on the porch when I pulled up in the buckboard with my pony tied behind. Sam and Ray were at her side, hopeful grins on their faces. Ray spoke for the two of them. "Can we go into town with you, Davy?"

"We ain't been to town for a long time," Sam put in plaintively.

Remembering what Kate and the ranch hands had said about Roche's men, I shook my head. "Not this time. I don't know if we'll run into any trouble or not. If we do, I don't want you boys around. You hear?"

Ray grimaced. "Awww."

Sam shrugged. "That's okay, Ray. Don't worry. We can hunt squirrels instead."

"Now, hold on, you two. I got other plans for you today."

Kate looked at me in surprise.

I continued. "The tack room in the barn looks like a tornado hit it and some of the gear needs mending. I'd be much obliged if you'd tend to that while your sister and I are in town."

They stared at me defiantly, then looked up at Kate. For a moment, she hesitated, then nodded. "Do as Davy asks," she said. "He's our foreman, and you know what Pa always said."

The smaller boy grimaced. "Yeah. Do what you're told, and don't argue."

Grumbling, the two boys stomped down off the porch and headed for the barn.

Kate paused before climbing up onto the buck-board. "They're not going to like you for that."

I grinned as I clambered down from the buckboard. "Probably not, but I figure if Russell was here, he'd do the same thing." I swung into my saddle.

She hesitated before picking up the reins. A faint smile played over her thoughtful face. "Yes. I suppose he would."

There was a chill in the early morning air, a hint of the months to come, but the briskness of the morning charged me with excitement.

When we turned onto the main road, she called out over the thudding of hoofbeats. "You think we'll run into trouble?"

All I could do was shrug. "Like I told you, I covered all that with the sheriff yesterday. We're not looking for trouble, but we're not running from it. When we get there, you just march in like you owned the place. I'll be right beside you. Don't worry. Everything will work out just fine."

A grim smile spread over her lips. "I hope so."

From time to time during the trip into Crockett, Kate pointed out various homesteads and ranches, but for the most part, we said nothing.

The small village bustled with activity. Sheriff Swain sat in a chair outside the jail watching the wagons passing and small groups of cowpokes riding in and out. I nodded as we rode past. He nodded back, a grim expression on his face. "The sheriff seems like a good man," I said to Kate.

She pulled up in front of Roche's General Store. "He's always been fair to us."

The same rotund clerk who had waited on me two days earlier looked up from behind the counter when the bell on the door signaled he had customers. His eyes grew wide when he spotted Kate, but he quickly hid his surprise. The few strands of hair on his head were combed across his baldpate. "Well, good morning, Miss Kate. I haven't seen you in quite a spell," he said in a timorous voice.

"Good morning, Mister Ludden." She stopped at the counter and handed him a list. "I need some supplies."

Casting a wary glance up at me, he reluctantly took the list and studied it. "Ummm. Yep, you got quite a list here, Miss Kate. I don't know if we have all this."

I stepped forward. "Then we'll take what you have, Mister Ludden."

He frowned up at me. "I remember you. You're that stranger who come in here a couple days ago."

Kate broke in. "This is Davy Nelson. He's my new foreman."

"Oh, I see. Well, I—ah—" A sheen of perspiration covered his round face, making his bald head shiny.

I pointed to the list. "Just start stacking the items on the counter, and I'll haul them out to the buckboard." I grinned, but the smile belied the look in my eyes.

Calvin Ludden nodded nervously. "Yes, sir. But, I don't know." He pointed to the list in his hand.

The grin slid off my face. I stared coldly at him. "What is it you don't know, Mister Ludden? You do sell to the public, don't you?"

"Yes, but—"

"And we are the public, isn't that right, Mister Ludden?"

He stared frantically at the list, then turned his pleading eyes on Kate. "Yes, but—well, truth is, I've been told not to give you any more credit, Miss Kate."

At that moment, the bell on the door jingled. I looked around as a jasper wearing one of those Prince Albert frock coats came toward us, followed by Cooter Fain and George Millikin, neither of whom appeared nearly as belligerent as they had when they jumped me in the saloon.

Carl Roche, I told myself, taking in the jasper wearing his fancy vest and ruffled shirt beneath his frock coat. About my size, he looked soft, like he'd just stepped out of a hot bath, but the most noticeable feature about him was his bulbous nose with a wart on the tip.

He stopped a few feet from us and nodded to Kate. "Miss McCall."

Kate gave him a brief nod. "Mister Roche."

Roche looked past us to the clerk. "Any problem, Ludden?"

The portly man hemmed and hawed a moment before replying. "Ah, no sir, Mister Roche. It's just that Miss Kate has a list of supplies, and I didn't know if you wanted—I mean, if I should fill it or not."

Roche looked at me squarely. "Certainly. Fill the order. That's what we're here for."

"B-But, she wants credit, Mister Roche," Ludden blubbered.

A look of consternation erased the thin smile on Roche's face. "Credit? Did you say credit?"

Ludden nodded.

Roche turned to Kate, a sorrowful expression on his face. "I'm sorry, Miss McCall, but we must have cash."

For a moment, Kate stared at him in shock. "But, we've always had credit, and we've always paid it off."

With a deep sigh, he shook his head. "That was then, Miss McCall. The Bar M is three months in arrears on your bill here at the store, and you have two mortgage payments due to the bank within three months." He looked at me and shook his head slowly. "I don't see how they will be able to pay what they owe. I wish I could help, but it's just business."

I eyed him coldly, resisting the urge to push his fat nose back between his eyes. He smiled smugly, figuring he had us over the proverbial barrel.

Keeping my eyes fixed on his, I asked, "How much is the Bar M's bill?"

Kate looked up at me, puzzled.

His eyes never leaving mine, Roche said, "What's the Bar M's tab, Mister Ludden?"

Several seconds passed. I could hear the riffling of ledger pages. "Four hundred and seventy-three dollars, Mister Roche."

A smug grin curled Roche's lips.

I knew what he was thinking, but I had my own ace up my sleeve. Keeping my eyes fixed on his, I said over my shoulder. "Fill the order, Mister Ludden. We're paying cash."

Beside me, Kate gasped, and the smug grin on Roche's face crumbled into disbelief. I slipped out of my vest. While I fumbled to loosen the threads, I glanced up at Roche, then glared at Cooter and Millikin. "I reckon I'll have to find another place to keep my money now," I said, pulling out several green-backs. "There are those types who always have a hankering for another jasper's money."

Cooter glared at me. Millikin's face reddened.

I turned back to the counter. Kate grabbed my arm. "No, Davy. I can't let you do this. You don't—"

"You don't have any say about it, Kate. This is my doing." I counted out $473. "There you go, Mister Roche. The Bar M's tab is clear." I hooked my thumb at the sweating clerk. "Now, have your boy fill this list, and I'll pay you in cash."

I grinned at Roche who was visibly upset. "I hate to see you throw good money after bad, Cowboy."

A sly grin slid over my face. "I reckon it depends on the eye of the beholder as to what's good or bad, Mister Roche."

The expression on his face told me I'd made a mortal enemy.

Ten minutes later, the buckboard loaded with supplies, we headed out of Crockett. I caught a glimpse of Roche talking to two hombres at the hitching rail in front of the bank down the street. They were too far to make out their features, but not so far that I couldn't see one mount was a three-stockinged sorrel and the other, a blood bay with black points.

Sheriff Swain still sat in his chair. He nodded as we passed, and this time, he had a smile on his face.

Propping her heels on the mud board and resting her forearms on her knees, Kate played the reins gently as she headed the buckboard out the west road. She looked up at me. "I don't know how to thank you, Davy. I'll pay you back, somehow."

"Don't worry none about it. Things will work out, you'll see."

We rode without talking, the only sounds the rattling of the bouncing buckboard and the squeaking of saddle leather.

After a spell, I cleared my throat. "When is the next mortgage payment due?"

"January 1. Two and a half months."

I grimaced. "Not long. I've been pondering what we should do. The only money you got right now is running around on four legs. That's what we've got to take advantage of. This is a bad time of year for cattle, I reckon, but is there a market around here for them?"

Our road curved into a thick stand of pines. Before Kate could reply to my question, two masked riders burst out of the thick stand of trees, brandishing six-guns. "Rein up," one shouted.

Chapter Eight

Instantly I recognized the blood bay and three-stockinged sorrel.

While I had been a prisoner most of the war, I hadn't forgotten the lessons I'd learned those first two years. When attacked, respond instantly or face the consequences.

Even before the words of their challenge died out, I had shucked my big Colt and thumbed off four shots, knocking both jaspers from their saddles.

I leaped to the ground and kicked the groaning owl-hoots' handguns away, then ripped off their masks. I called out to Kate over my shoulder. "You know these two?"

Kate peered down from where she sat on the buckboard seat. She nodded jerkily. "Not their names, but they work for Carl Roche."

One was unconscious, shot in the chest. The other struggled to sit up, holding his left arm. I touched the muzzle of my Colt to his chin and tilted his head back. "Who sent you?"

He groaned. "I think you busted my arm."

"I'll bust more than that if you don't tell me who sent you."

"Nobody." He clutched his arm and shook his head. "Someone in the saloon said you was carrying a wad of money, that's all, honest."

"You're a liar." I cocked the Colt.

He grimaced against the pain. "No, I ain't, Mister, honest."

My voice cold as ice, I growled between clenched teeth. "I'm asking you once more. Who sent you?"

He glared up at me, a smirk on his lips. "I told you. Nob—"

I slammed the muzzle of my Colt against his injured arm. He screamed, a chilling shriek. "I won't ask again. Next time, I'll put a .44 slug through your head."

Blubbering, his words ran together. "Roche. It was Roche. He sent us. I swear. Don't hit me again. Please don't hit me again."

Holstering my Colt, I shook my head in disgust. "I oughtta finish the job on you two. Your pard there might be finished anyway, but you get your worthless carcasses back to Crockett and tell Roche that whatever he does to us, we can do to him, in spades. You understand?"

His face twisted in pain, he nodded jerkily.

"And if I ever find either of you two doing any harm to the McCalls or the Bar M, I'll put pills in your stomach that you'll have a heap of trouble digesting. In fact, I were you," I added, "I'd get myself all doctored up and head somewhere away from here. I might be sorely tempted to give you six feet of dirt were I to see you again."

I glanced at Kate as I swung into the saddle. Her slender face had paled.

Several times throughout the remainder of the ride, I saw Kate looking at me from the corner of my eye. Before we reached the drive to the ranch, I turned to her. "I told you, Kate. I don't run from a fight, and I won't back down. If you're having second thoughts about me, now's the time."

She studied me for several moments. She shook her head slowly. "No, Davy. I'm not having any second thoughts."

Sam and Ray were playing mumble peg when we drove in. I waved them over to help us unload the wagon. Smoke limped out to meet us just as Speck rode in.

When Kate told them of the incident on the road, Speck frowned and shook his head. Shifting his mouthful of tobacco to his cheek so he could talk, he said, "Roche ain't going to like that one bit. He ain't used to folks bucking him." He arched an eyebrow. "He won't take what you done to them lying down."

Kate eyed Speck resolutely. "We knew bucking Roche was not going to be easy."

Speck grunted. He looked at me. "You can count on something. And it ain't going to be no church social." He punctuated his prediction with a stream of tobacco.

Smoke agreed. "You can blasted well bet on it, Davy."

I threw a bag of flour over my shoulder. "We'll worry about that when the time comes. Now, let's get us this buckboard unloaded."

After we finished unloading the supplies and unhitching the horses, a single rider on a sorrel horse rode up to the main house and climbed down. He knocked on the door.

Speck peered through the corral rails. "Take a look. Ain't that old man Martin?"

Kate squinted across the hardpan. "Sure is. Wonder what he's doing over here. His place is back east a few miles."

The hackles on the back of my neck bristled. Brushing the dust off my denims, I nodded to Kate. "Reckon we need to find out. Speck, you come along too. Sam, Ray, hang the rigging up in the tack room."

The older man stomped down off the porch when he

spotted the three of us coming to meet him. He raised a hand. "Howdy, Kate, Speck." He glanced at the corrals. "Hope I didn't take you away from nothing important."

"Howdy, Luke. Just doing a little work in the barn." She nodded to me. "This is my new foreman, Davy Nelson. Davy this is Luke Martin, a good friend." She smiled brightly. "What brings you out here? You care for some coffee or a drink of water?"

He shook his head, a worried frown on his craggy face. "No thanks, Kate. I come to warn you. I just come from town. Word says that two of Roche's boys was shot up. Roche was mighty upset, so upset that I wouldn't at all be surprised if you folks get some unexpected visitors. Maybe tonight."

Speck grunted. "What did I tell you, Davy?"

The old rancher looked around warily. "I'm heading home through the woods. I don't cotton to running into them on the road. Roche would know for sure I warned you."

Kate stepped forward and laid her hand on his arm. "Don't worry, Luke. No one will hear it from us."

"That took guts," I muttered as we watched the older man ride away.

"Luke Martin has always been a good friend. I don't want anything to happen to him."

Grinning at Speck, I said, "Looks like you were right."

"Right about what?" I glanced around as Smoke limped up, drying his grizzled hands on a damp dishtowel.

"Reckon we can expect some visitors tonight," Speck announced.

The old cook grunted. "Roche uses them nightriders like a shotgun."

"How's that?" His remark puzzled me.

"Ain't no proof, but rumor has it that he was the one that had the Jinks' barn burned down one night. Old Bob Jinks sold out the next week and moved back east."

I glanced around the ranch, then grinned at the three of them.

Speck frowned. "I don't see nothing to grin about."

My smile grew wider. "You fret too much, Speck. Let the nightriders come. We'll have a nice little surprise for them."

Kate shoved her hat to the back of her head. "What kind of surprise?"

"Yeah. I'm a tad curious myself," drawled Smoke.

I made a sweeping gesture to the ranch with my arm. "Take a look."

"What the Sam Hill we looking at?" Speck groused.

"The ranch." I explained. "Russell and me did this just about every night, of course, not on as big a scale as we'll have to do, but it was effective."

Smoke snorted. "What the tarnation we looking at?"

"Look how the ranch is laid out. Stands of pine in

front and back, hills to the east, and the flood plain to the west." I looked around at them. "In those first days of the war, Russell and me learned real fast to rig up at night what we called silent sentries. From time to time, those Yanks would try to sneak in on us, but we got in the habit of stringing ropes with pieces of metal tied to them around the camp. That's what we'll do here."

Speck snorted. "Take a heap of rope to string it all around the place."

"No." I shook my head. "If we have any late-night visitors, they're not going to climb up and down those hills to the east or try to come up the steep slope from the flood plain. Like all skulking cowards, they'll want to come in fast and get out fast, before we can react."

Kate's eyes lit. "So what you're saying is that we string ropes across the two roads coming into the ranch?"

"Exactly. String 'em up at night, take 'em down in the morning. I figure three or four across the front road and the same across the back road ought to do the job." I nodded to Sam and Ray. "Smoke, you and the boys get us tin cans, tin plates, anything we can tie to the ropes that'll make a commotion. Bring them out to the barn while Speck and me get the rope."

When Otsie Bets and Red rode in, the six of us were working on the ropes. I explained what we were up to, and they pitched in to help us finish up. From time to time, I glanced at Otsie. He seemed a little distracted, like he had something on his mind.

Back to the north, a line of dark clouds rolled over the horizon. "Looks like weather," Kate said. "Maybe—" she hesitated.

I chuckled. "Maybe they won't come? They will. Count on it."

Late afternoon, a fine drizzle brought falling temperatures as Kate and her brothers joined us at the chuck house for supper. Smoke cooked up a special beef stew with extra thick gravy and pieces of sourdough biscuits mixed in.

For the first few minutes, we all were so busy poking the grub down our gullets, nobody said a word. Finally, Speck managed to mumble a question around a mouthful of stew. "When do we put up the ropes, Davy?"

"Right after supper. Red, you, and Otsie string up three ropes across the back road. Speck and me will take care of the front one."

"Can't we help?" Ray looked up at me hopefully.

I winked at Kate. "Sure you can, son. You go with Red and Otsie. Sam, you want to go with me and Speck?"

"You bet."

As we rose from the table, Otsie spoke up. "After we string the ropes, I reckon I'll ride into town for a drink or two. I'll be back by midnight."

I studied him a moment. He glanced at the floor. "Tell you what, Otsie," I said, my voice low and cool.

"I'd feel better if you stayed here tonight." The others looked at me in surprise. I continued. "I'm by nature a suspicious jasper. Now, they might come tonight, or they may not, but if you were to ride out, and Roche's boys somehow learned about the ropes—well, sir, I'd have to figure it came from you."

Otsie did his best to look surprised, then chagrined. "You accusing me of working for Roche on the sly?"

I grinned and shook my head. "Why, no, Otsie. But, things happen. Words slip out accidental like. You just hang around here tonight and none of those accidents will happen."

He opened his mouth to retort, but then clapped it shut. "If that's what you want," he replied, his words brusque and curt.

"That's what I want. Now, let's string those ropes."

The fine drizzle continued to fall. We donned our slickers, and with Sam tagging along Speck and I strung our ropes across the road. When Speck finished knotting the last rope, I rolled a cigarette and tossed the bag to him. "Otsie been here long?"

Guarding his match against the drizzle, Speck touched the flame to his cigarette. "About three years, I reckon. Why?"

"Just wondering," I said with a shrug.

"You think he's hooked up with Roche?"

I pondered his question. "Have you ever started to step over a log, and something told you not to? And when you looked, there was a big fat copperhead or rattler lying in the shade of the log?"

He frowned. "Not that I can remember."

"Well, that's kind of the feeling I get when I'm around Otsie. I might be wrong, but I reckon time will tell." I flipped my cigarette to the hardpan and ground it under my boot. "I figure tonight we'd best grab a tarp and throw our bedrolls in the trees by the road. My guess is that if they come most of the shooting will be up at the front, so that's you and me. Red and Otsie can watch the back road. Make certain your rifle is fully loaded. If those old boys come in tonight, we want to provide them with a proper greeting."

Speck stopped and turned to me. "You mean, shoot to kill?"

"Over their heads. Let's just give them a good scare."

Chapter Nine

Around midnight the drizzle abated, leaving a chill in the air. The heavy cloud cover broke apart from time to time, letting the stars peek through.

I had dozed once or twice, but the rest of the time I lay snug in my blankets listening to the drizzle pattering on the tarp enclosing me and my bedroll.

And then, a short while after the drizzle passed, a new sound reached my ears—the thundering of hooves. I threw the tarp off my head and jumped to my feet, at the same time whispering harshly to Speck. "They're coming!"

"I hear 'em," the lanky cowpoke muttered.

Pressing up against a thick pine, I peered in the direction of the pounding hooves, squinting in an effort to penetrate the darkness. I could see nothing, but the sounds grew nearer.

I cocked the hammer on my '66 Winchester and waited. The ground beneath my feet began to vibrate. "Get ready," I whispered, glad I had insisted Sam return to the main house.

"I'm ready as I'll ever be."

The hoof beats grew louder, drawing nearer and nearer until finally it seemed they were right on top of us.

And then a horse squealed and a man screamed in the middle of the clamor of clanging tin, "What the—" A hard thud followed.

"Now!" I shouted.

Speck and I began firing blindly into the treetops across the road.

Frightened men cursed; horses whinnied and squealed; three or four shots were fired in our direction.

"Back, back," a voice shouted. "We run into a trap."

Another voice called out. "Cooter, Cooter! Where are you?"

"Shut up and get out of there, or we'll leave you behind."

Later, in the parlor of the main house, we told Kate and the others what had taken place.

Speck cleared his throat. "And there ain't no question, Miss Kate, that Roche is behind it. We heard some hombre call out Cooter Fain's name."

Still fully dressed, Kate turned to me. "Now what?"

I arched an eyebrow. "I'd say we just told Carl Roche exactly where we stand, wouldn't you?"

She and Speck grinned at each other. "I certainly would," she replied. "I certainly would."

"In spades." Smoke cackled.

"That was just the first step," I said to Speck as we slogged through the mud back to the bunkhouse with our bedrolls under our arms.

"What do you mean?"

I veered off toward the barn. "I'm going into town."

"Tonight? Why?"

"I'll tell you later. Anyone should ask, tell them I'm watching the road in case the nightriders come back. Especially Otsie Bets."

"But, they ain't. You know that. We put a big scare in them."

"Like you just said, you know that, and I know it, but I've got a message for Mister Carl Roche, and I plan to deliver it tonight."

"What kind of message?"

"You'll find out."

"Well, then, I reckon I'll ride along with you," he announced, heading to the barn with me.

"Could be trouble."

He chuckled. "That's my first name, Trouble Webster."

"All right then, Trouble, it's your choice. I'll tell

Red we're both watching the road. If everything goes without a hitch, we'll be back in time for Smoke's flapjacks."

We pushed our horses hard. From time to time a passing shower swept over us punctuated by patches of clear sky. We reined up on the outskirts of Crockett around three A.M. soaked and chilled. The town was dark, lit only by the light of stars shining through the momentary break in the clouds. "We'll leave our ponies over there," I whispered, indicating a cluster of pines behind the livery.

Speck dismounted and tied his horse to the trunk of a pine. "Now will you tell me what you've got in mind?"

I glanced over my shoulder as I climbed down off my bay. "I figure on burning down the blacksmith shop," I replied matter-of-factly.

He gaped at me. "What?"

"Let's go," I whispered, hurrying around the back of the livery. "If I remember right, the blacksmith shop is right next door."

"But—"

I slipped through the darkness to the blacksmith shop, pausing at the corner to peer up and down the main street. "Would you take a look at that," I whispered.

Speck pushed up beside me. "What are we looking at?"

"The bank. The lights are on. And take a look at the

horses at the hitching rail. I'd say Mister Carl Roche is getting a report of the night's business."

Speck chuckled. "And probably pretty doggone mad about it too."

"Well, let's go," I said, slipping around the corner and gliding through the shadows toward the large double doors. I lowered the lock bar, and we darted inside.

"It's darker than the inside of a cow in here," Speck muttered.

"Stay at the door and keep an eye on the street. I'll take care of things in here." I struck a match, and in the far corner of the shop I found what I was looking for: a five-gallon container of coal oil. Removing the cap, I soaked my neckerchief and stuffed it in the opening, leaving a few inches dangling down the side of the can.

I hurried back to the forge and held my hand over the coals. Still warm. I began pumping the bellows.

"What's going on?" Speck whispered anxiously.

"Building a fire." The coals came to life, and within a few minutes they were cherry red. "You ready to run?" I called out.

"Just give the word."

The light from the hot coals illuminated the shop with a soft orange glow. "Get ready. We'll probably have only a minute or so to get away from here." By now, the bed of coals had turned almost yellow, their heat threatening to blister my skin.

I stopped pumping and grabbed the can of coal oil.

I sat the tin container in the middle of the coals and bolted for the door. We slid around the corner of the shop and skidded through the mud to our ponies.

Seconds later we were racing down the Centerville road. "Remember, Speck. This is between you and me. Don't even tell Kate," I called out above the thundering of hooves.

A minute passed, then two. I was beginning to worry that someone had discovered my little bomb.

Suddenly, a soft whoosh rolled across the countryside and the sky over Crockett lit up like daytime.

Before sunrise the next morning, we hauled down the ropes and stashed them in the barn. I sent the hands out to select stock to push to Huntsville, a hundred miles or so to the south of the Bar M. The market for cattle was weak—only seven to ten dollars a head—but Kate and I decided if we could move five hundred heads, she'd have enough to pay up the mortgage with a tidy sum left over.

Sometime around mid-morning, Sheriff Swain rode in as Kate and me were finishing up making a list of supplies we would need for the drive to Huntsville. He wore a Confederate great coat against the biting wind.

Kate invited the sheriff in for a mug of steaming coffee, coffee so strong it could do the work of a six-horse team. "What brings you out this way, Sheriff?"

He removed his great coat and sat at the round oak

table, placing his battered hat on the table. "Just riding past," he drawled.

"Oh?" She glanced at me and gave a sly wink as she poured him some coffee.

He sipped the torrid black mixture and smacked his lips. "I swear, Kate, ain't nobody can touch you when it comes to good, hot-range coffee."

"That's nice of you to say, Sheriff, but I'm sure you didn't ride all the way out here to pay compliments to my coffee. And," she added, "it's too raw a day for a leisurely ride."

He grinned. "Yes, ma'am. You're right. Truth is, I heard roundabout you all had some trouble out here last night."

Kate and I exchanged puzzled looks. "Trouble?" I innocently replied. "Not that I know of, Sheriff. What about you, Kate?"

Arching her eyebrows, she shook her head. "No. What are you driving at, Sheriff?"

"Well, Kate, story I got was that Carl Roche sent two of his men out here with an offer for your place and you—or one of your hands—" he added hastily, "shot at them. One got his nose busted when his horse reared back, and the other ended up with a broken arm."

I spoke up. "I'm afraid Mister Roche might have got hold of some bad whiskey, Sheriff. That's the only thing I can figure would have him come up with a story like that."

He eyed me narrowly. "So, you're saying no one came out here last night."

Trying to appear as innocent as possible, I nodded. "That's what I'm saying."

He looked from me to Kate suspiciously, then hooked his thumb over his shoulder. "When I rode in the front road, I saw what looked like blood in the mud."

I turned to Kate. "Probably that drifter who came through yesterday morning drunker 'n' a skunk. Why, he was so drunk, he fell off his horse and busted his nose. Bled all over the place."

From the glitter in Kate's eyes, I could see she was trying to suppress her laughter. "Davy's right, Sheriff. The drifter passed out in the barn. He didn't wake up until yesterday afternoon, and then he rode off. Heading to Centerville, if I'm not mistaken," she added for good measure.

He studied us suspiciously. "Well, that being the case, I don't reckon either of you know nothing about Roche's blacksmith shop burning down early this morning. Probably still smoking."

Kate's surprise was genuine. "Who did it?"

Swain shrugged. "That's what I'm trying to find out."

"Well, Sheriff. None of my men left the ranch last night. They were all here."

He looked at me with a shrewd gleam in his eye. "That include you?"

"Reckon I wouldn't make a liar out of Miss Kate, Sheriff."

"You had trouble with some of Roche's boys in town a few days back."

"Yep, but I got back at them."

He chuckled. "I know."

I shook my head. "So some jasper burned Roche's blacksmith down, huh?"

Swain sipped the last of his coffee and set the cup on the coffee table. "Yep."

Clucking my tongue, I drawled, "Reckon he's mighty lucky that jasper didn't burn his bank instead of the blacksmith, isn't he, Sheriff?"

The sheriff studied me through narrowed eyes that reflected his suspicion. "Yep, I reckon so," he replied, rising and slipping into his great coat with the cape falling over his shoulders.

I nodded to the coat. "Cavalry, huh?"

He grimaced briefly. "Yep. Second Cavalry, State Troops, back in '63 and '64."

"Heard of you boys. Good outfit."

A wry grin split his weathered face. "For all the good it done us."

"That's what all wars are good for. Tell you what, Sheriff. If you don't believe us about nobody leaving here last night, you're welcome to ask the other punchers. They're out on the southeast range cropping ears."

"Cropping ears? You plan on a drive this time of year?" he asked incredulously.

I tried to cover my blunder. "Nope. Just sorting stock for a spring drive. But like I said, you're welcome to ride out and talk to any of our punchers."

A faint grin ticked up one side of his lips. "I might just do that, Mister Nelson. They might have a better memory."

Chapter Ten

We watched from the window as Sheriff Swain huddled down in his great coat against the chill, rode out the north road. "You think he believed us?"

"Must have," I replied. "Looks to me like he's heading back to town without questioning the boys."

Her brows knit in question, Kate searched my face. "Was everyone here last night?"

With a chuckle, I replied, "You heard what I told the sheriff. I sure wouldn't want to make you a liar."

Her eyes narrowed, and a cryptic smile played over her lips. "Don't hand me that. Did you have anything to do with the blacksmith shop?"

I stroked my chin. "Anything?"

"Yes."

"Suppose I said, not anything, but everything?" Her

eyes grew wide, and I continued. "You remember what I told those two owlhoots who tried to hold us up? I told them to tell Roche that whatever he gave us, I'd give him." I set my jaw and narrowed my eyes. "That's exactly what I did." She said nothing, just looked up at me in disbelief. "I told you out on the road yesterday, Kate, that I don't run from a fight, and I won't back down. I'm a peaceable gent, but I don't allow nobody to run over me or mine or to push me around. Now, if that gives you cause to worry, then tell me, because, the truth is, things won't be getting better around here until either me or Roche are gone from this part of the woods."

To her credit, she didn't hesitate. She smiled broadly and stuck out her hand. "Let's buck the tiger, friend."

It was my time to be surprised. "Buck the tiger? Now, where did a little ranch girl learn words like that?"

Her smile turned provocative. "There's a lot about me you don't know, Mister Nelson. A whole lot."

For the next few days I kept all punchers out on the range, selecting and marking stock, at the same time expecting some sort of retaliation from Carl Roche. To my surprise, all remained quiet. And that made me even more uneasy.

I still had my doubts about Bets. Although he never mentioned going into town again, I had the feeling he'd bolt if I gave him half a chance.

* * *

"We don't need the chuck wagon, Smoke," I said one day when he asked if he were going on the drive. "Shouldn't take us more than a week. We'll carry our grub in our saddlebags. I've lived on worse than hot coffee and jerky. Fix us up some biscuits and bacon. We'll make do with that."

"But, Davy," he argued. "A cattle drive ain't no cattle drive without no chuck wagon."

"Maybe so, Smoke, but I need you as a puncher. I plan to leave the boys here with Kate. I promise, next spring when we head beeves north, we'll take your chuck wagon. But this time, do what I ask, if you think you can still fork a horse." I grinned.

His eyes blazed fire. "You young whippersnapper. Give me a bronc, and I'll teach you a lesson."

By now, we were approaching November. More and more small cold fronts had blown in, bringing chilling rain and dropping temperatures.

That day before we pulled out, we gathered the stock south of the ranch above the flood plain. While driving the cows across the plain below would be a heap easier than over the hills and around the woods, the grass on the plain was thinner, less nutritious. The beeves would be more content, less likely to bolt where the graze was better.

As Speck and me sat on our ponies that last night staring at the starlit hills off to the south, he muttered, "I ain't worried about the drive, Davy, as much as I am the river. I never liked pushing herds over a river."

I laughed and slapped him lightly on the shoulder. "Don't worry none, Speck. I've pushed just about every kind of animal there is across rivers. I'll push you across too."

We moved out next morning before the sun came up. There were five of us: me, Red, Speck, Bets, and Smoke. I put Speck at point, Smoke and Red at swing, and me and Bets brought up drag. Around midday, my leg started aching.

I'd herded beeves enough to know that we had to push them hard the first day of a drive to tire them out so that all those ornery critters wanted to do the first night was sleep.

When we hauled up that first day, I guessed we'd made a good fifteen miles.

The day's drive must have been hard enough on the beeves, for when I took the first shift at nighthawking, the cows didn't appear spooky or nervous, just grateful for a chance to rest.

Three hours later, I awakened Speck. "Your turn to sing to them," I joked.

"What are they like?"

"Quiet. Red will spell you in a couple hours." I deliberately left Otsie Bets out of nighthawking because I still had reservations about him.

I crawled into my blankets, grateful to give my throbbing leg a chance to rest.

It seemed as if I'd just gone to sleep when a hand on my shoulder shook me awake. "Davy, Davy! Wake up."

My eyes popped open, and I stared up at Smoke, the shadows cast by the fire playing over his face. "Huh? What's wrong?"

"Bets is gone. He pulled foot out of here on his shift."

I sat up abruptly, muttering a curse. I climbed to my feet, hobbling a moment. I peered into the gray of false dawn. "When? He didn't have a shift."

The old man shrugged, and pointed his empty tin cup at the herd. "Got no idea. I got up and put the coffee on. I was starting to pour a cup when it hit me I hadn't heard no lullabying out at the herd. I wandered out there, and he wasn't nowhere to be seen. Ain't nobody out there."

"Blast!" I looked around. Red was sawing logs. I clenched my teeth. He was supposed to have the last shift. I touched the toe of my boot to his shoulder.

He blinked his eyes. "Huh? Time to get up?"

"Where's Bets? What are you doing here? You was supposed to take the last shift."

Blinking, he sat up, a confused look on his face. "What do you mean where's Bets? Nighthawking, that's where."

"No, he ain't," Smoke retorted.

Red looked up sharply. "What do you mean, he ain't? He took my shift. He said he wasn't sleepy, and that would give him something to do."

By now the commotion had awakened Speck. "What's the fuss?"

"The fuss is that Bets has run out on us," I said.

"So?" Speck piped up. "Ain't no loss as far as I'm concerned."

I eyed his coldly. "I'm not worried about losing him. I'm worried about who he might tell. The reason I kept us all on the ranch, especially Bets, was so Roche wouldn't hear about the drive. You can wager the last thing he wants is for Kate to get a herd through."

"You figure Bets is working for Roche?" Smoke asked.

"I don't know, but if Bets gets enough whiskey in him, he'll probably say something he shouldn't. And I'll bet you a ten dollar bill whatever he says about the Bar M will get back to Roche."

Red shook his head. "I'm sorry, Davy. I didn't figure it'd hurt nothing. Ask the boys. I sleep like a rock. Sometimes you got to kick me in the rear to wake me up."

I waved at him. "Forget it, Red. No way you could know. Besides, I might be wrong about the man. Let's just saddle up and get these beeves on the trail."

By the time we saddled up, Smoke had the coffee boiling. I gulped a cup against the cold, managing to burn the roof of my mouth. That and cold biscuits and jerky would have to do me until nighttime.

We drove hard that day, helped by a strong north wind and a few scattered snow showers. I had mixed feelings about the snow. Such weather added substantial difficulty to our job. On the other hand, cattle normally drifted away from the snow, so riding drag, I didn't have as many contrary beeves to turn back into the herd.

Night came early under the snow-leadened clouds, and just before dark, we reached the S-bend in the Trinity River where we planned to cross next morning. The beeves were content to mill about in the shelter of the oak and hickory trees lining the river, picking up graze where they could or simply standing in one place chewing their cud.

Red took the first shift while Speck, Smoke, and me hunkered around a blazing fire in front of a canvas fly strung between two oaks for a windbreak. Overhead, we stretched another fly for a flimsy roof. The snow was light but steady. The roof began to sag, so in a nearby windfall of huge oaks and hickory deposited in a shallow gully by the last flood, we found a long branch, which we used to prop up the middle of the roof so the snow would slide off.

Smoke shaved some jerky into a small pot and boiled us up a jerky broth that sure warmed us as it went down. I massaged my gimpy leg by the fire, trying to ease the throbbing.

Speck shivered. "I ain't lying when I say that I don't look forward to that river crossing tomorrow morning, Davy. It's blasted cold now. We're going to freeze when we come out of that river soaking wet and have to face this cold."

He was right, but I didn't see that we had a choice. "You got any suggestions, Speck? I reckon I'm open to them."

He studied me with a dry expression for a moment, then shook his head. "Nope. Don't reckon I do. This here is the best crossing for miles."

"How deep is it?"

"Has a gravel bottom. I reckon it's around four feet deep."

"At least we ain't going to have to swim," Smoke put in.

I cleared my throat. "I got no more wish to get frozen to the saddle than you boys. String your boots and socks over your saddle. We'll get our legs wet up to about our knees when we push the herd across. Once on the other side, we'll slip the dry socks and boots back on."

Speck frowned. "I don't wear no socks."

With a grin, I replied, "At least your boots'll be dry."

"What about the cows?" Smoke asked.

"Don't fret over them. Once over the river, we'll push them hard enough to warm them up real good." I grimaced as a sharp pain ran up my leg.

Speck leaned back on his saddle and snuggled down

in his Mackinaw. "You know something, boys, it's almost right snug in here. At least we don't have far to go for firewood," he said, nodding to the windfall.

"My leg pains me something fierce when weather gets bad," Smoke remarked when he saw my rubbing my leg.

I chuckled. "That's the cross us cripples bear, Smoke."

He cackled.

Speck looked around at me, a curious expression on his slender face. "Whereabouts you from, Davy? That is if you don't mind me asking."

With a shrug, I replied, "I got nothing to hide. Up north on the Red River. A little town named Honey Grove."

Taking a sip of his coffee, Speck remarked, "Small, you say?"

I chuckled. "Small enough you could fit it in your back pocket and have enough room left over for a six-horse team."

Chuckling, Smoke grunted, "Reckon that's small."

"Yep. Its one claim to fame is that Davy Crockett came through there on the way to Bexar, down at the Alamo."

Speck perked up. "Crockett? You don't say?"

"Yes, sir. In fact, that's how I come by my name. When Crockett and his Tennesseans stopped at Honey Grove, the town threw them a shindig. According to my Pa, him and Davy got into a shooting match. Pa got beat out, but not by much. He took a liking to Crockett, so much so that when he got word of the Alamo on the day I was born, he named me David William Nelson."

Speck shook his head. "Well, I swan. What's the *William* stand for? Your Pa's name?"

"Nope. After Travis—William Barrett Travis."

"Well I swan," Speck muttered again. "I reckon that is some kind of—ah, what do they call it when two unlikely things happen?"

"Coincidence?" I frowned, not following the lanky cowpoke's drift.

"Yeah. Coincidence. You was named for Davy Crockett just like our town was named for Crockett." He grinned broadly. "Maybe something is telling you to hang around here. Why—"

Several gunshots in rapid succession cut off his words.

Chapter Eleven

We jumped to our feet as the staccato cracks of rifles and handguns mixed with the bellowing of frightened cows and wild shouts. The dreaded thunder of pounding hooves rolled through the darkness toward us.

"Stampede!" Smoke shouted.

"They're coming this way," Speck yelled.

I spun on my heel, and the sudden movement sent a sharp pain through my gimpy leg. I cried out through clenched teeth. "Quick, the windfall."

Smoke stumbled over a saddle and sprawled on the ground near the fire. I yanked him to his feet and shoved him down the gully toward the windfall. "Get in there. Hurry."

I leaped behind the thick trunk of a dead oak into

the middle of the windfall and landed right on top of Smoke in a tangle of arms and legs.

The herd separated, passing on either side of the windfall.

Within brief minutes, it was over. In the distance the thunder of hooves and wild yells faded.

Smoke pushed and shoved at me. "Blast it, Davy, get your feet outta my face."

I squirmed around and poked my head up above the thick trunk of the dead tree. The darkness was so thick I couldn't see my hand in front of my nose.

Then I remembered Speck. A cold chill ran up my spine. Only me and Smoke make it to the windfall. I called out, "Speck! Speck!"

Far above a choked voice replied, "Up here."

I peered into the darkness above. "Where?"

"Here!" he shouted. "Wherever that is. You and Smoke hurt?"

"No."

At that moment, some of the scattered coals from our fire flared, offering just enough illumination for us to find our way back to our camp, which was now in shambles.

Speck muttered a few angry curses as we reached the flickering flames. "Those blasted owlhoots got out of here before I could get a shot at even one of them."

Using the toe of my boot, I scraped some of the coals into a pile. "Get some wood," I said, heading back to the windfall.

"They got all our cows, looks like," Smoke grumbled.

"And horses," Speck growled. "They tore loose from the picket rope."

I looked around in alarm. "Red!"

With the help of torches, we found Red beside an ancient pecan tree. I knelt at his side.

Speck grimaced. "Is he dead?"

The stampeding herd had messed him up something fierce. I ran my hand under his mud-caked coat to check for a heartbeat. I nodded without looking up. "Afraid so."

"I don't see how them beeves could have took old Red by surprise," Smoke whispered. "He was too good a cowman."

"That isn't what did it," I said, holding my hand in the light of Speck's torch.

Smoke's old eyes grew cold. "Blood."

I opened Red's coat. The torchlight fell across a bloody patch over his heart. I unbuttoned his shirt to reveal a hole in his chest.

Smoke cursed. "Them no-good—" And he reeled off a stream of profanity that must have taken him a lifetime to perfect.

We carried Red back to our camp. We found one of the canvas flies and rigged a crude windbreak against the snow. For the remainder of the night we huddled around the fire, praying for daylight.

Speck narrowed his eyes and looked at me. "You think Roche was behind all this?"

"Makes sense to me. Who else had anything to gain?"

Smoke nodded. "There ain't no question in my mind that lowlife skunk is behind tonight. He's greedy for the Bar M, and he won't stop at nothing to get his hands on it."

"Why the Bar M and not the other ranches?"

"Because," Speck replied, "the Bar M has the river, and Roche has dreams of a steamboat business hauling goods along the river all the way down to the Gulf of Mexico."

"Yep," Smoke snorted. "He already owns most of the town and half a dozen ranches. Like I said, he's greedy. He wants everything."

A silence fell over the camp. After several minutes, Speck cleared his throat. "We ain't going to find their trail in this snow," he mumbled, holding his hands to the fire and staring into the flames. "Reckon you know that, don't you, Davy?"

"Reckon I do, Speck. Reckon I do. But we've got to try."

Speck was right. At first light, we began searching for signs of the stampede. Inside the treeline the snow had not obliterated all sign, but a few hundred yards east of camp, where the herd left the trees and headed across the prairie, the snow covered the tracks.

I muttered a curse. "Reckon that does it." I looked at Speck and Smoke. "All that's left to do now is to head back to the ranch."

Smoke nodded in the direction of our camp. "What about Red?"

"Best we bury him," Speck replied.

"How do you plan on doing that? We ain't got no shovels."

"Wrap him in canvas and pull logs over him until we get back with shovels," I said. "If we get lucky, maybe we'll stumble across a couple of our ponies. We could be back here in two days."

Speck shrugged. "Fine with me."

Smoke struck out for the camp. "No sense in wasting daylight."

We wrapped Red in the canvas fly, tied it tightly with rope, then stacked logs over him. "That ought to keep off the varmints for a couple days," Speck drawled when we stepped back to survey our handiwork.

"He always gave a good day's work for his pay," Smoke whispered.

I nodded. "Reckon that's about the best you can say about any jasper."

At that moment, we heard a horse whinny. Upriver a hundred yards or so, two of our ponies stood staring at us, their reins dragging the ground. One was my bay; the other, Smoke's sorrel.

* * *

Smoke and me took turns hauling Speck. We pushed hard, hoping our horses could stand up to the rigors of a brutal ride, knowing that every minute the chances of finding our herd were diminishing.

We reached the Bar M around midnight.

Kate took the news hard. Her lips quivered, and tears gathered in her eyes. She clenched her hands into fists. After a few minutes of silence, she said, "You men get some sleep. You must be exhausted. In the morning we'll decide what to do next."

"I don't want no sleep." Speck exclaimed. "I say we ride into town and put Carl Roche in a pine box."

"I'm for that," Smoke added.

"Hold on, boys. Where's the proof? We got none." I paused and shook my head. "As much as I'd like to do the same thing, we've got to have proof. And we'll have it if we can connect the rustling to Roche. Kate's right. We need some sleep, but in the morning, Speck and me are heading back to bury Red, then get on the trail of those rustlers. Maybe we can get some of the herd back or find evidence that Roche was behind it."

A faint smile of gratitude played over Kate's lips. She struggled to hold back the tears. All she could do was nod.

We slept a couple hours, and well before the sun rose we were riding south, carrying shovels and a few days' grub along with extra boxes of cartridges for our six-guns and Winchesters.

By mid-afternoon, all the snow had melted, leaving a thick morass of watery mud. "If it's like this at the river," I mumbled, "there won't be anything to follow."

Speck grunted his agreement.

We reached our old camp in the shank of the afternoon and by sundown, had planted Red. Afterward, we ate cold venison and biscuits and washed it all down with hot coffee. As a treat, Smoke had whipped up some hound's ears and whirliup—thin sourdough fried crisp in the shape of a dog's ear and covered with a whirliup sauce of sugar and water with chopped dried apples. The dessert was cold, but we put ourselves around it just like it was hot off the stove.

Speck lay back on his saddle and patted his belly. "That old man sure did hisself good with this grub tonight."

"He did that," I replied.

We pulled out early next morning. I tried telling myself that we would find enough sign to follow, but when we rode out on the prairie, I saw instantly that my worst fears had been realized. All tracks had been erased by the snow.

Speck muttered a curse. "Now what?"

"Well, they were heading east when they pushed out of the trees. Let's us ride half a day or so to the east. See what we can see."

"Fine by me," he replied, kicking his gray into a gentle lope.

All we found for the next hour was mud and more

mud, and then in the distance we spotted a dark object on the ground, which turned out to be a dead cow.

"One of ours," I muttered when we reined up.

"Yep. Right ear over-split," he said, gesturing to the V-shaped notch in the top of the cow's ear. "One of ours for sure."

With a click of my tongue, I urged my bay into a lope. "Let's see if we can find more."

An hour later, we spotted two more dead cows, and then our hopes surged when we found about eight or ten heads grazing on the thin grass. We pushed them ahead of us. Below the crest of the next hill, we came up to twenty or thirty more of our stock.

By nightfall, we had put together a small herd of about forty-five to fifty of our beeves.

They were restless. "Hungry," Speck observed.

Surveying the countryside around us, I replied, "Not much out here for them to graze on. Come morning, we need to keep them moving at a good pace. Don't give them a chance to think or they might decide to head out in all directions.

That night we took turns watching the beeves.

Over a cup of steaming six-shooter coffee next morning, I proposed we push the herd on to Huntsville. "We're over halfway. Pick up a few dollars. Not much, but enough to keep us going until we can come up with another idea."

Speck chuckled. "I reckon you're bound and determined to get me in that river, huh?"

Laughing, I replied, "Just remember to tie your boots over your saddle."

He nodded, and after breaking camp, we headed the herd west.

That night we camped at our old camp, and next morning pushed the small herd across the Trinity. I did the pushing while Speck stayed downriver to keep the stock from breaking away with the current.

I grimaced against the icy water that seemed to be paralyzing my right leg.

By nightfall we arrived in Huntsville.

Next morning, we headed back to the Bar M, $500 in my pocket.

After crossing the river mid-afternoon, I gestured in the direction of Crockett to the northeast. "Where is Roche's ranch?"

"You mean from Crockett?"

"Yes."

"Due south of town, about an hour's ride. Why?"

I studied Speck thoughtfully. "I've got an idea."

"Huh?"

"Here." I slipped the roll of bills from my pocket and handed it to him. "You ride on in and give this to Kate."

"But what are you going to do?"

"What's Roche's brand?"

Speck frowned. "Circle CR. Why do you want to know?"

"Because I'm going to ride over and take a look at his herd."

"You're what?" Speck's eyes grew wider than Smoke's pie pans.

I said nothing, just nodded.

"You'll get yourself shot dead."

Reining away from his gray, I grinned. "They'll have to do it fast. I'll be in and out before anyone knows I'm around."

"You're crazier than a drunk chicken."

"Tell Kate I'll be in sometime tomorrow."

Speck shook his head, his thin face taut with worry. "I'm telling you, Davy. You're going to get yourself killed over there."

Chapter Twelve

I put the bay into a walking two-step, a mile-eating gait that wouldn't tire him so easily, saving his strength just in case I needed a burst of speed. For the most part, I remained close to the stands of pine and oak that dotted the rolling countryside, ready to duck inside should I spot another rider.

Once, I saw two cowpokes heading my way so I slipped into a thick stand of pine and dismounted. I pinched the bay's nostrils so he wouldn't whinny when the other ponies passed. The two trotted past not thirty feet from me. I waited until they were out of sight, then continued my eastward journey.

I passed over the Lazy Three range, the brand of which was the figure three lying on its side, and the Tumbling T, a T tilted sideways.

Then I reached the Circle CR. Behind me, the sun was only minutes from the horizon. I spotted a few dozen beeves grazing a quarter of a mile or so across the undulating meadows. I headed toward them, but just as I drew close enough to inspect them for the over-split right ear, a shout off to my left pulled me up.

Two cowboys burst out of a copse of pine racing toward me, flailing their ponies for all they were worth. I didn't know if I should turn tail and run or bluff my way. I decided to bluff. The only hombres I knew who worked for Roche were Cooter and Millikin. I flipped the leather loop off the hammer of my big Colt and slid it up and down in the holster a couple times.

Two hardcases with a week's beard skidded up to me. They looked like they belonged on a wanted poster. One of them growled. "You're on private property, Cowboy."

"What are you doing here?" the second one snarled.

Relieved that I had never seen the two, I shrugged. "Just drifting. A cowpoke back on the trail said there might be work at a town named Crockett."

The two studied me narrowly, digesting my story. "Well," the first one said, "there ain't no work around here, so you best keep on riding—" he nodded to the east, "—in that direction."

I glanced at the sun. "Be dark soon. Any objection if I camp in that patch of trees you boys come from? I'll ride out at first light."

The second one spat out. "You best ride, Mister. Don't stop for the next hour. Like we said, you're on private property."

I studied the two hardcases. I had no doubt I could blow each of them out of the saddle before either had a chance to draw, but I had grown tired of killing. Besides, they had given me the perfect opportunity to inspect Roche's beeves. "East, you say?" I pointed directly toward the grazing stock.

"You heard right. Right through the middle of them cows yonder."

Nodding, I touched my finger to the brim of my Stetson and, not wanting to spook the cattle, headed east at a walk. To my disappointment as I ambled through the stock, I spotted no over-split right ears, but I also stumbled across several with freshly cropped right ears, an easy modification of the over-split. All a rustler had to do was continue the V-split at the top of the ear and sever the tip, leaving half an ear. Then I spotted the brand on those with the cropped ears, the Box M. I grimaced, and then I realized how simple it would be to change the McCall brand, the Bar M, to a Box M.

I wanted to take a closer look, but two sets of eyes were on my back, so I kept moving, squinting into the growing darkness.

And then I spotted a cow that convinced me Roche was behind the rustling. The top half of the crop had healed, but the bottom half was still bloody. Someone had changed the over-split to a full crop. I would have bet the moon that someone worked for Carl Roche.

Without looking back, I rode until after dark before pulling into a motte of oak. Inside the stand of oak, it was dark as a stack of black cats. I dismounted and, feeling my way, tied my pony to a low limb, after which I gnawed on some jerky and waited. I figured that as soon as the two hardcases saw me disappear, they'd turn back.

I gave them another hour, then headed back to the Bar M. I had plans to make.

Next morning around the breakfast table, I suggested Kate and I report the rustling to the sheriff. "We can take the buckboard and pick up supplies."

Ray McCall looked up at his big sister. "Can me and Sam ride into town with you, Kate, huh? Please."

Kate glanced at me. I turned to Ray. "Not this time, boy. Things are mighty touchy around here. I'd rest easier if you and Sam stayed here. Besides, why aren't you in school today?"

The young boy gave a frustrated grunt. "It's Saturday."

"Tell you what then. You and Sam give Speck a hand with the cattle while we're gone, and we'll bring you back some licorice."

"And a sarsaparilla?" Sam put in.

I chuckled. "And a sarsaparilla."

"You going to tell Sheriff Swain that Roche is behind it?" Smoke asked.

"Nope, but I am going to tell him about the altered ear markings on some of Roche's cattle."

"That'll sure stir Roche up, you accusing him of rustling," Speck remarked.

With an expression of innocence on my face, I replied, "Who's accusing him of rustling? All I'm saying is that I discovered beeves with altered ear crops on his range. I don't know how they got there."

"How do you explain the Box M brand on them cows?" Smoke asked.

"They could have used a running iron to add the other three sides of the box. It was too dark to see if the brands were fresh or not, but maybe with the sheriff, we'll have a chance to look."

Sheriff Swain grew more and more intent as he listened to the events of the rustling, the death of Red Tucker, and my discovery of the altered ear crops in Roche's herd. "Now understand, Sheriff, I'm not accusing Mister Roche of rustling. All I said was I found altered ear crops among his stock, some that looked to be no more than a day old."

He mulled my remarks a few seconds. Finally, he pushed to his feet and reached for his hat on the hat rack. "Suppose we just go over and see what Mister Roche has to say about this."

* * *

Carl Roche rose from behind his desk at the bank when we entered his office and smiled. He extended his hand. "Sheriff Swain. A pleasure to see you. And Miss McCall." He offered Kate his hand. His smile flickered and his eyes grew cold when he looked at me. "And Mister Nelson." He took a step back and surveyed us. "What do I owe the privilege of your visit?" He gestured to the chairs in front of his shiny desk.

The sheriff shook his head. "This won't take long, Mister Roche. Might be nothing to it."

Roche arched an eyebrow. "To what, may I ask?"

"Kate here had five hundred head of stock rustled. Red Tucker, you know him—"

"Certainly. Good man," the banker replied, his voice oily smooth.

"Well, Red was killed. The snow wiped out the trail, but Nelson here found some altered ear crops mixed in with the Circle CR brand."

Roche shot me a look filled with knives. In a calm voice, he asked, "May I ask Mister Nelson what he was doing on my range?"

I spoke up. "I didn't know it was your range, Roche. I was riding and looking. I rode through a couple other ranges, one with a three laying on its side."

"That's the Lazy Three," Swain said.

"And another with a T turned at an angle."

"The Tumbling T."

I nodded. "Before we moved the cattle, we put an

over-split notch in the right ear of every cow. On your range I found some with cropped right ears."

Roche frowned. "I don't understand. If you were looking for over-splits, I don't see why you would be concerned about a cropped ear." Beneath his patronizing tone, I sensed a tightly controlled anger.

"Because, a simple flick of a knife will turn an over-split into a crop, and I noticed on several cows, the top of the crop was healed, but the bottom was still bloody."

His frown deepened. He turned to the sheriff. "I don't understand what he means, Sheriff. What difference would it make if it was bloody or not?"

I glanced at Kate, puzzled. Was Roche that ignorant about cattle? The expression on her face told me her thoughts were drifting in the same direction.

Swain explained. "That means that someone recently altered the original notch, Mister Roche."

Roche's face hardened with resentment. His bulbous nose seemed to grow red, and he glared at me. "Are you accusing me of stealing McCall cattle?"

"Nope. All I'm saying is that you have some altered ear notches on your range."

He studied me coldly, then in a cold voice asked, "Is the Bar M the only one around Crockett that marks their stock with over-split notches?"

I looked at Kate. She shrugged. "I don't know," I replied.

A smug grin ticked up the sides of his lips. "Nor do

I, Mister Nelson." He looked back at the sheriff and continued. "I do not doubt Mister Nelson's veracity, Sheriff. I—"

Swain grunted. "His ver—what?"

Roche hesitated, pained tolerance on the features of his soft face. "Veracity. Ah, the truthfulness of Mister Nelson's story. If he says he saw altered notches, I believe him."

Roche's willing acceptance of my accusations took me aback. He opened his desk drawer and pulled out a sheet of paper. "Day before yesterday, I purchased a hundred head of stock from a rancher by the name of—let me see—" He paused to scan the document in his hand. "Ah, here it is, Chester Morgan. Here's the bill of sale," he added in a smug voice. He handed the bill of sale to Sheriff Swain. "You can see for yourself."

Swain read the bill of sale and nodded. "Who is this Morgan gent, Mister Roche?"

"He's from Homer over in Angelina County. And you can see the bill of sale is notarized by my secretary, Mister Ezekiel Watts."

The sheriff looked at me. "Well, Mister Nelson?"

"What was the brand?"

Roche frowned. "Sorry, I don't remember, but it's on the bill of sale you're holding, Sheriff."

Swain glanced at the document. "The Box M."

"Were those the brands you saw, Mister Nelson?"

Nodding slowly, I replied, "Yes."

The sheriff handed Roche the bill of sale, then turned to me. "Anything else, Mister Nelson?"

I stared at Roche, reading the smugness glittering in his black eyes. He had beaten me, and he knew he had beaten me. Even if the brands on the cows had been altered, he had a bill of sale that incriminated the seller, not the buyer. "Well, Sheriff, I suppose my next step is to ride over to Homer and see Mister Morgan. See what he knows about all this."

Roche nodded his approval. "An excellent idea, Mister Nelson. If by some chance I have come into stolen property without being aware of it, I'll certainly do all I can to set matters straight."

Swain touched his fingers to the brim of his hat. "Much obliged for your time, Mister Roche."

After picking up our supplies, Kate and I headed back to the Bar M. "He's mighty slick," I mumbled as we bounced over the road back to the ranch. "But I still think he's behind it."

Kate looked at me in surprise. "What about the bill of sale?"

"Easy to forge. And the notary is his secretary." I drew a deep breath. "I'll say this for Carl Roche, he threw up a nice little roadblock for us this time."

"What's next?"

"First thing in the morning, I'm riding to Homer. I want to pay Chester Morgan a visit."

*   *   *

When I reached the small village of Homer the next evening, I tied up in front of the Buckskin Saloon. Inside, I bellied up to the bar, which was nothing more than rough planks laid over wooden beer barrels. Half a dozen or so coal oil lamps hung from the ceiling, scarcely breaking apart the shadows in the small room.

"Howdy, Stranger," the bartender said in a deep voice. "What'll it be?"

"A beer."

He drew one from a barrel behind the bar, building a frothy head. He sat it in front of me. "That'll be a dime. What else?"

I slapped a dime on the bar. "How do I find a jasper by the name of Chester Morgan?"

He paused with his hand on the dime and studied me with eyes sunk deep in his angular face. "You a friend of his?"

"Nope. Never met the jasper. Just want to talk to him."

"You're a tad late, Mister," he replied, picking up the dime. "Chester Morgan is dead."

Chapter Thirteen

I choked on my beer. When I got over my coughing fit, I looked at the bartender in disbelief. "He's what?"

"Yep." He nodded, leaning back against the sideboard and building a cigarette, unperturbed by Morgan's death. "Burned hisself up last night. Reckon he got drunk and passed out. He was bad about that." He paused and looked at me. "Getting drunk and passing out, that is."

All I could do was stare at him. Finally, I found my voice. "Did you know him?"

He grunted and shrugged. "Everybody knew Ches. He had a little shack a piece out of town."

"A shack? I thought he had a ranch around here, the Box M."

The bartender looked at me in amusement. "A

ranch? Morgan? Naw. Did odd jobs. Some figured maybe he stole a few cows here and there, but the sheriff never could throw a loop on him."

I tried to sort my thoughts. Could it be possible this Morgan was the one who rustled the herd, then sold a hundred head to Roche? If so, where was the rest of the herd? Maybe he had sold them to various ranches along the way from the Trinity to Homer. "Have you seen him around in the last week or so?"

He pondered my question a moment, then shook his head. "Last time was a couple weeks back." He turned to straighten the beer mugs on the sideboard in front of the mirror behind the bar.

"Is there a Box M ranch around here that you know of?"

"Not that I know of," he replied over his shoulder.

"You sure?"

He turned to face me. "Stranger, I been behind this bar fifteen years. I know every ranch for thirty miles. You can believe me when I say there ain't no Box M around Homer."

I spent the night camped outside of town and awakened next morning to an overcast sky from which showers of freezing drizzle and light snow began to fall. I took time to fortify myself with a cup of steaming coffee before heading back to Crockett.

Because of the overcast, night came early. It was full dark when I spotted the lights of Crockett. A thin layer of snow covered the ground. I reined up in front of the sheriff's office. The shades were drawn. I stomped inside, shivering. My gimpy leg was bothering me something fierce.

Sheriff Swain looked up in surprise when he saw me. A second gent was with him, a stranger, a bald-headed stranger who, though seated, appeared to be about knee-high to a June bug and thin as the bug's legs.

"Mind if I warm myself, inside and out?" I asked, heading directly to the potbellied stove with a coffee pot on top. The aroma of fresh coffee made my mouth water.

"Go right ahead, Mister Nelson. Looks like you can use it. You just getting back from Homer?"

I nodded, pausing in front of the red-belly of the stove, luxuriating in the heat driving the chill from my lanky frame. My leg ached like old Satan had stuck his pitchfork in it. The Yank doctor had said it would. The slug had shattered my shinbone. "Especially in cold weather," he had warned me.

I shifted my weight to my left leg, trying to gain at least a modicum of relief from the sharp pains racing up and down my right one. "Yep," I replied. "Just got back right this minute." I glanced over my shoulder at the two. Both men were watching me. Swain cleared his throat. "Mister Nelson, this here is Lum Bishop. Lum's the postmaster here in Crockett." He grinned at the small man, and good-naturedly added, "He was made for the job. He don't have to do nothing but sit on his rump and pass out the mail."

Lum grinned at me. "That's better than a sheriff who does nothing but sit out in front of his office everyday. At least I get some work done."

Sheriff Swain snorted.

"Pleased to me you, Lum," I said, rubbing my hands together briskly. "I'm Davy Nelson. I work out at—"

The postmaster cut me off. "I know. Sheriff told me." He shook his head. "Like I told Jess here, if I was a betting man, I'd place a hundred to one odds that there ain't no way you can keep the Bar M from Carl Roche's greedy hands."

I glanced at the sheriff and grinned. "Sheriff's been talking about me, huh?"

Lum chuckled. "Stranger comes to town and bucks Carl Roche? Why, Son, that's pure fodder for gossip. The whole town's talking, and it galls Banker Roche mighty bad."

Swain pointed to the coffee pot. "Bring us some coffee, Davy. We could all use a cup against the cold." He fumbled in his desk and came up with three tin cups and a half-full bottle of Old Orchard whiskey.

After filling the cups and sitting the pot back on the stove, I took the chair next to the postmaster, gingerly stretching my right leg out straight.

While Swain splashed a dollop or two of whiskey into our cups, Lum gestured to my leg. "Get that during the war?"

"Yep," I sipped the coffee and groaned with satisfaction. "I can't remember when anything tasted so good."

Sadness filled his face. "I lost my boy in the war. Vicksburg."

For a moment, the horrors of the war flooded back, but I pushed them aside. I had once told myself that over time the memories would fade, but they hadn't. "Sorry, Lum. I reckon everyone got hurt."

"Except them blasted Yankee carpetbaggers," Sheriff Swain muttered.

I looked around in surprise at the bitterness in his voice. For several seconds, no one spoke. Finally, Swain said, "What happened in Homer?"

Briefly, I related what I had learned.

The sheriff grimaced in disgust. "Truth is, that's about what I expected. I had hopes though," he added. "But, I'm not surprised."

"Me neither," Lum said.

Puzzled, I said, "I rode over there hoping to find something that proved Roche was behind the rustling. You two sound like you were hoping the same thing."

"We were," Sheriff Swain replied.

"In spades," Lum said.

I forced an awkward grin. "You could have fooled me, Sheriff."

"Why? Because I treat Roche the same as everybody else? That's what a sheriff is supposed to do. That don't mean I have to like it, but it's my sworn duty."

The tiny postmaster leaned forward. "Look, Davy. Three quarters of this town would like to see Roche gone, me and the sheriff included, but the man's too slick. He knows all the angles."

"He stays inside the law on everything he does," Swain said. "That's why you're not going to find any proof that he was behind rustling Bar M stock." He paused to pour another splash of whiskey into our cups. "I wish we could soak his worthless Yankee hide, but as much as I hate to say it, I'm afraid Carl Roche is too smart for us."

I sat staring at the two men for several moments. "Whereabouts is Roche from?"

Swain frowned. "What do you mean?"

"Where does he hail from? Where was he before he came here?"

"Got no idea."

Lum spoke up. "I don't know where he's from, but every so often, he gets mail from a lawyer in St. Louis."

"Any place else?"

The small man thought a moment, then shook his head. "Nope. Only St. Louis."

I grinned. "That's where we start."

"Huh?" Swain stared at me, baffled.

"Look, Sheriff. You know as well as me there's many a jasper out in this part of the country who's got a spot in his past he doesn't want anyone to know about. Now, I'm not saying Roche is one of those, but maybe it's worth a try to contact the law in St. Louis and see what they have to say about him. He might be as clean as a baby's leg, but then again, maybe he won't. It isn't much of a chance, but it's worth the price of a letter."

Lum Bishop and Sheriff Swain looked at each other as if to say why they hadn't thought of the idea before. "Davy's right, Jess. It's worth a try," said Lum.

"It certainly is. Why—"

A faint bump against the wall near the side window cut Sheriff Swain off. We stared at each other a moment, then the sheriff strode to the window and pulled the shade aside. "I would have sworn I heard something," he muttered.

On a shelf behind the sheriff's desk was a lantern. I lit it and went outside. The snow continued to fall as I headed for the side of the jail with Lum and the sheriff on my heels. I froze at the corner of the brick building.

"What's wrong?" Lum muttered.

"Look," I said, holding the lantern closer to the ground where the lightly falling snow was beginning to fill in fresh boot prints. "And I'll lay you odds these tracks lead to the window."

They did, and as we stood staring at them, Sheriff Swain cursed. "I reckon I best get that letter off first thing in the morning. "'Pears to me, Mister Carl Roche is on to our plans."

* * *

I bunked in the single cell of the jail that night, but I slept only in bits and pieces, depressed by my wasted trip to Homer, skeptical of our attempt to find any skeletons in Carl Roche's closet, and puzzling over just how Bar M could come up with the funds to pay off the bank.

Well before sunrise, I rose. Sheriff Swain had the coffee on. We pulled our chairs up to the stove, savoring the heat radiating from the cherry red stove. "You still planning on writing that letter, Sheriff?"

He grunted and using his cup as a pointer, indicated his desk. "Done wrote it. Got up during the night. I'm taking it over to Lum as soon as I finish this coffee."

I nodded slowly, trying to suppress the sense of helplessness flooding over me. "Maybe we'll get lucky."

He snorted. "Maybe, but I reckon I'm enough of a doubter not to count on it."

After draining the last of my coffee, I rose, buttoned my Mackinaw and tugged my Stetson down on my head. I eyed the sheriff a moment, then offered my hand. "You best take care, Sheriff. If someone did hear us last night and takes the word to Roche, he might start getting ideas."

A crooked grin curled Sheriff Swain's lips. He shook my hand firmly. "You're the one who needs to keep his eyes open. Roche pretty much had things his way until you came along."

*   *   *

The sky had cleared, the air was crisp and sharp, and a smooth coat of white blanketed the countryside. Strange, I thought, how something could be so downright beautiful in the midst of an ugly world.

I rode into the ranch at mid-morning and reined up at the main house. Before I could dismount, Kate rushed out onto the porch, a smile beaming on her face. "Davy! You're all right." She sounded as if she half-expected me to come back in a pine box.

"Reckon I'm just fine, Kate." I patted my belly. "I'll be doing a heap better after I put myself around some of old Smoke's grub."

Pausing before climbing the steps, I frowned up at her, spying the dark circles under her eyes. "You been sick?"

She shook her head emphatically. "No. I'm fine." She took a step back. "Come on in. I have some hot coffee and a plate of Smoke's fresh fried doughnuts in the parlor. I'll send one of the boys to fetch Smoke and Speck."

I followed her into the parlor where Mrs. McCall rocked slowly at the side of the hearth, her unseeing eyes fixed on the dancing flames, lost in a world of her own. Removing my Mackinaw, I greeted her as I always did, knowing I would get no response. "Morning, Mrs. McCall."

Kate set a cup of six-shooter coffee and the plate of doughnuts on the coffee table in front of the couch.

I tore into them eagerly, dunking one in my coffee and gulping down half of it without chewing it much more than two or three times. Kate sat across the table from me.

About that time, Speck, Smoke, and the boys came in, all excited.

"Well, what did you find out?" Speck demanded.

I shook my head. "Not good." I told them the same story I had related to Sheriff Swain and Lum Bishop. As I talked, the hopeful expressions on their faces turned to dismay.

Kate closed her eyes and leaned back in her chair. Finally, she opened them and looked at me. "So, you're saying we don't have a chance?"

All four of them stared at me. I could read the desperation in their faces. "Maybe one chance. A small one."

The hope my words brought to their faces faded quickly when I told them about the sheriff's letter to St. Louis. "It isn't much of a chance, but it's something."

Depressed, Kate replied, "But not much."

"No. We'd be crazy to count on it." I drew a deep breath and released it slowly. "That means it's up to us to find some means to pay the mortgage."

Speck spoke up. "What about trying to move more cattle to Huntsville?"

Kate caught her breath. "I don't think so."

"Speck might have something there, Kate," I said. "You'd need to hire a couple more cowpokes."

She laughed bitterly. "I tried to hire some after we lost Red, but everyone is too scared of Roche."

A knock at the door startled us. Kate sent Ray to answer it, and he returned moments later followed by a wiry old cowpoke who looked to be in his fifties. His weathered skin was pulled taut over his angular face, and he was so bowlegged a calf could run through his legs without disturbing a hair. "This is Mister Fuller. His buckboard broke down on the main road and needs help. His wife is down there with it."

By the time we slid the butcher knife wheel on Albert Fuller's buckboard and dug up a locknut for the wheel, it was close to dark. Kate invited him and Mrs. Fuller to supper and offered them a bedroom in the main house, which the older couple eagerly accepted.

Around the supper table later that night, Fuller told us that he had just purchased a ranch over in Centerville and he and his wife were on their way to settle in and then find some cattle to stock it. "But," he said, "I was right disappointed in the price of beeves back in Crockett."

Kate looked at me in disbelief, then smiled at the rancher. "Mister Fuller, I think I can help you."

He arched an eyebrow. "Oh?"

"I have prime stock here. How many head do you want?"

He shrugged. "Two hundred or so."

"What price did you have in mind?"

"Back in town, they said twenty-five dollars was the going price for good stock."

"How about fifteen?"

"On delivery?"

Kate glanced at me, arching her eyebrows in question. I nodded. She continued. "Take a look at them in the morning, and if you want to make a deal, we'll deliver."

"How long do you reckon it'll take you to get them to me?"

"Not long, Mister Fuller," I replied. "It's only twenty-five miles or so. Two days. Three at the most."

He rose to his feet and extended his hand to Kate. "You have a deal, Miss McCall. My place is a couple miles south of Centerville. It's the Crossed Diamond." He glanced at his wife who smiled demurely. "Me and Ma will be waiting for you."

Chapter Fourteen

We were happier than a romp of weasels in a hen-house. With the three thousand for the cattle, the Bar M could meet its obligation at the bank even though we were stripping down the herd considerably.

The next day turned out warm. Kate and the boys pitched in to help gather the two hundred head. The older boy, Ray, did a good day's work, but then he was thirteen, the age when most western boys became men.

Kate and me watched as he pushed four or five beeves into the herd. "He'll make a good cowman," I said.

She beamed. "He takes after Russ."

Keeping my eyes on the boy, I said, "It'll be a short drive. If you've got no objection, I'd like to take Ray with us."

Kate looked around at me in surprise, but I kept my eyes on the boy. She hesitated. "I—I don't know. I hadn't even thought about that."

I turned to her. "He'll do fine, Kate."

Her face took on a worried look, and she chewed on her bottom lip. "I don't know. He's so young."

"Thirteen. I remember Russell saying that when he was that age, he was herding stock for your Pa."

"I know, but—" She looked up at me. "Can't you and Speck and Smoke handle the herd?"

"Reckon we can. This is just a chance for the boy to start growing up." I paused a moment. "It's natural not wanting to turn him loose, especially after Russell. But, it's going to happen sooner or later, whether you want it to or not, Kate."

She stared after her brother, considering my words for several seconds. Her face went hard, and she looked me squarely in the eye. "No. I won't let him go. Not this time."

With a slight shrug, I conceded. "He'll be disappointed."

"I don't care."

I knew how she must feel. She lost one brother, and she didn't want to take a chance on losing another. I couldn't blame her.

Kate and eight-year-old Sam were standing on the porch the next morning when I pulled up at the hitching rail. "We should be back in three days. You all going to be all right?"

"Don't worry about us," she replied with a crooked smile.

I glanced around. "Where's Ray? Figured he be here to see us off."

Disgust crinkled her face. "Inside. Sulking." The fire in her eyes dared me to say "I told you so."

Discretion kept my lips sealed.

Speck called out from the corral. "Time to head out, Davy."

Reining my bay around, I called out over my shoulder. "See you two in a few days."

We swam the herd across the river without incident. The three of us managed the beeves with Smoke at point, and me and Speck doing double duty at flank and drag.

We pushed the herd hard, making camp that night only ten miles out of Centerville. Speck nighthawked the first shift. I planned to relieve him at midnight. I was leaning against the trunk of an oak enjoying the heat of the fire when I heard branches cracking in the dark night beyond the camp.

Quickly, I shucked my Colt and crouched behind a scrub of oak. Smoke followed suit on the other side of the fire. Whoever the rider was, he didn't know his range manners, which prescribed that upon first spotting a campfire at night, you helloed the camp. Not observing such etiquette had sent many a jasper up that golden stairway to heaven.

Finally a tremulous voice broke the darkness. "Davy! It's me, Ray McCall."

Surprised, I called out. "Ray? Is that you?" Sometimes I had a penchant for dumb questions. This was one of those times. On the other hand, his sudden arrival after his sister's adamant refusal muddled my thinking.

"Come on in, boy," Smoke called out.

Ray rode into the firelight, a bedroll tied to the cantle of his saddle and a Henry repeater in the rifle boot. He wore a heavy jacket. I holstered my Colt as he reined up and stared down at us.

Shaking my head, I said, "What the Sam Hill are you doing out here? I didn't think your sister would let you come."

He gulped, then blurted out, "She doesn't know I'm here."

My jaw hit the ground.

Smoke snorted. "Lordy, Lordy, boy. You going to catch the tanning of your life when you get back."

The young man set his jaw. "I don't care. I helped gather the beef, so I figure I was entitled to go along with you all."

I rolled my eyes. "Well, get down and tend your pony. Then squat and fill your belly."

He remained in his saddle. "Can I stay?"

Smoke and me looked at each other, momentarily at a loss for words. Finally, I replied. "Son, you put me between the rock and the hard place. I sure don't plan on sending you back by yourself. I reckon you might as well ride on into Centerville with us tomorrow, and then we'll head back together.

A broad grin leaped to his face, and he quickly dismounted.

Just after noon the next day, we spotted Centerville. By mid-afternoon, we rode onto the Crossed Diamond spread. "Hold the stock here, boys," I said. "I'll fetch Mister Fuller, and he can tell us where he wants the herd."

I figured after collecting the three thousand, we would try to make it back to the Bar M tonight. I wasn't anxious to make camp with that much money in my pocket.

The Crossed Diamond needed work. A couple of sound-looking horses stared at me over the opera rail of the corral. I spotted his buckboard beside the barn, which also needed a heap of work. I wrapped my reins around the hitching rail in front of the main house and stomped up on the porch. I knocked.

Several moments passed. I knocked a second time, and as I did, the door opened. My eyes bulged when I saw Albert Fuller. The smaller man looked up at me through swollen eyes. He wore a split lip and a dark purple bruise on his cheekbone.

I stepped back, startled.

Resisting my curiosity, I simply announced, "Your cattle is here, Mister Fuller. You want to take a look?"

His eyes shifted nervously. He swallowed hard. He cleared his throat. "I—ah—I changed my mind. I don't want the herd."

I stared at him in disbelief. In a choked voice, I said, "What did you say?"

He ran his tongue over his battered lips. "I said I changed my mind. I don't want the cattle."

I couldn't believe what I was hearing. "But, you agreed. You shook on it."

He dropped his chin to his sunken chest, then slowly raised his eyes to meet mine. "I know I shook on it, but I had to change my mind. That's my right," he added, trying to sound belligerent but failing miserably. He fumbled in a vest pocket and pulled out a folded greenback. "Here. Maybe this will make up some for the trouble."

Numbed by our sudden reversal of fortune, I took the greenback. By now, my brain had absorbed just what had taken place. My ears burned, and I felt the fires of anger flaring in my chest. In a cold, hard voice, I demanded, "Who got to you, Fuller? Carl Roche?"

He shook his head. "Nobody got to me."

"You didn't get your face messed up like that falling off your horse. Who was it?"

"Nobody," he exclaimed, shaking his head. He stepped back and started to close the door. Infuriated, I kicked it open with the heel of my boot and slung the bill in his face. "You keep your money. I don't want nothing from a coward."

I muttered obscenities all the way back to the herd where I had to throw my arms around Smoke to keep him from going back to the main house and stomping Albert Fuller to a grease spot.

Instead of the elation we expected to feel after selling the cattle, the two-day ride back to the ranch was filled with gloom and hopelessness. I was frustrated, and I was mad. Carl Roche was pushing us around just like we were pushing the cattle.

By the time we came in sight of the ranch, my frustration had bloomed into raw anger. I didn't know what I was going to do, but I wasn't about to stand around and do nothing. I'd been kicked in the teeth enough.

But, when we reached the ranch, I took another kick in the teeth.

Chapter Fifteen

Stoically, Kate fought back the tears when I told her about our failed trip. She shook her head and whispered. "It's all over now."

I didn't want to give her any false hope, but I couldn't still the anger coursing through my veins. "Not yet. Not for another month."

"We could always try Huntsville again," Speck opined.

She looked up at me, her large brown eyes filled with pain. "That's not all, Davy."

I let out a deep sigh. "There's worse?"

"Sheriff Swain is dead."

"Dead?" I stared at her in shock.

"Worse than that. Cooter Fain is now sheriff. He

came out here yesterday and said unless we paid the mortgage, we had to be out by the first of January."

"Yeah," Sam exclaimed, "and his men shot five of our cows."

"They what?" I looked around sharply.

He nodded emphatically. "After they left, I heard shots. I ran to the top of the hill and saw the riders shooting the cows. And they was laughing about it."

Speck's eyes blazed. He laid his hand on his hogleg. "I say it's time to ride into town and settle this once and for all."

"No," I said. "You do that and all that will be settled will be you under six feet of dirt. That's playing right into Roche's hands."

"So what do we do?" Smoke snapped. "We can't squat here and do nothing. I might be gettin' long in the tooth, but I ain't never been the kind to turn the other cheek."

I studied the old man several seconds, and then I remembered something Kate had told me that first night. I looked at her. "You say your Pa was killed on the way back from town where he was supposed to have made a mortgage payment?"

"Yes, but Roche claimed Pa gambled the money away."

"And you don't believe that?"

"No. Pa didn't gamble."

"It's the surefire truth, Davy," Smoke put in.

Speck added his two cents. "They're both right. Her Pa, old Ed, why he wouldn't even sit in a poker game in the bunkhouse when we was playing just for beans."

"You say he lost it in Roche's Saloon, huh?"

Kate nodded. "That's what they claim."

"What about the bartender? If your Pa was there, he would have seen him."

Sneering, Kate replied, "He'll say what Roche wants to hear."

I stared at my scarred knuckles, at the same time pondering her remarks.

She saw the studied expression on my face. "Why? You have something in mind?" Kate looked at me hopefully.

"I reckon right now Roche figures he's got us where he wants us. We try to push another herd of beeves, he'll steal it. We can't hire the manpower to fight him off, so I suppose we'll just have to do it ourselves."

Her brows knit. "Ourselves? Are you serious?"

"Yes, Ma'am, but not in the way you think."

Dismay filled her eyes when she understood the intent in my reply. "You can't whip Roche, Davy. He has too many men."

I searched deep into her eyes. "What choice do we have, Kate? You think Russell would have turned tail and run?"

For a moment, her eyes were hard like flint, but quickly softened. She replied in resignation, "No. I don't suppose he would."

"Do you have any kin around that you can take your Ma and boys to?"

She frowned. "A cousin down at Sumter about twenty miles or so south of here. Why?"

"We can't beat Roche playing the game he's picked, so we're going to make him play ours."

"I don't understand." Speck frowned.

"Roche has all the cards in his favor, and now he has the sheriff. You think Cooter Fain won't come back out here throwing his weight around?"

Slowly nodding, Speck grunted, "Suppose so."

"I know so." I turned to Smoke and fixed him with a hard stare. "I want you to take Kate and the rest of the family to Sumter. Me and Speck will stay behind."

Smoke growled. "If there be any fighting, I ain't running from it."

I grinned at the old man. "Getting Kate and the family away from here and keeping them safe is just as important as fighting. More so."

Kate took a step forward. "But you and Speck can't hold them off if they come back. There'll be too many of them."

"I don't plan on fighting them off. Speck and me will disappear into the forests, and we'll hit Roche when he least expects it." I paused at the puzzled frown on her face. "There was a bunch of Johnny Rebs who did that very thing to us. They hit and ran. By the time we got where we thought they were, they had disappeared."

Kate protested. "Disappear into the forest?" She gestured to the room about her. "What about the ranch? If you and Speck leave, there won't be anyone to take care of things."

"Sure there will," I replied. "Roche."

Speck looked at me in surprise. "What do you mean, Roche?"

"Simple. Roche wants this place. Once he discovers we've abandoned it, there's no reason to shoot it up. Just cost him more to repair it." I grinned at Kate. "When we get back, it'll be in as good a shape as when we left. Maybe even better."

Within an hour, the buckboard full with Mrs. McCall sitting in her rocker in the back and Kate and Smoke on the seat disappeared over the hill behind the ranch buildings. The boys rode alongside on their ponies.

At the top of the hill, they all pulled up and waved.

We waved back. After they disappeared over the pine-topped crest, Speck shivered and looked around the deserted ranch. "Sure lonely here, just the two of us. Kind of spooky."

"Won't be for long, Speck. Now, let's load up our saddlebags with grub and cartridges. We got a heap of work to do. I just hope we can get it done before we run out of time."

He grimaced. "How much time you reckon we got?"

With a crooked grin, I replied. "Until Roche runs us down, or until we drive him out."

Casting a glance over his shoulder as we rode away from the ranch leading a packhorse, the lanky cowpoke muttered, "Hate to leave the place deserted."

"Reckon I know what you mean. Like I said, I don't figure Roche will let Cooter do anything to it once he finds out we've all gone. He wants it, and I reckon he'd prefer it in one piece."

The last of my concerns was the deserted ranch. Our part of the country hadn't grown so callous that passing strangers would not observe the etiquette of the west. If they were hungry, they'd whip themselves up something to eat. If they needed to swap horses, they'd leave us a note. They'd treat the ranch as if it were their own. The cowboy might seem like a savage to easterners, but there was a different code of honor in the west much more rigid than back east.

Speck glanced at the coils of rope I had insisted we tie to the packhorse, eight coils each altogether. "Where are we heading and what do you have in mind with all them ropes?"

I nodded to the thick stand of oaks half a mile to the north. "We'll stay in the woods. Never the same place twice. As far as the ropes are concerned, never can tell when one might come in handy. Remember the nightriders?"

A crooked grin played over his lean face. "Reckon I do. Reckon they do too. So, now what you got in mind?"

"The way I see it, we have two choices. Either we figure out how we can prove Ed McCall made the mortgage payment, or we run Roche out of town."

The frown on his face deepened. "How do we go about either one? Roche sure ain't going to keep no receipts laying around. He probably tore it up as soon as he ordered someone—probably that blasted Cooter Fain—to shoot old Ed down like a dog."

"You're probably right, but I'm figuring on making certain of that fact." With a shrug, I added, "I've seen many a smart man outsmart himself."

"Not Roche," he replied skeptically. "He's too slick."

"We'll see."

"I suppose you know," he said with a laconic drawl. "We could get ourselves killed dead."

I chuckled. "Not me. I still haven't seen California yet."

As we rode, I explained what I had in mind. "I can't figure out how we can learn if McCall paid the mortgage or not. Until we can figure out a way, the smartest thing for us to do is whittle down his manpower."

He looked around at me. "You that good with that Colt?"

"That isn't what I had in mind. I'm not anxious to

kill anybody, so the next best way to get rid of some-one would be to scare the pants off them. That's why we need some dynamite."

He looked at me in surprise. "Dynamite?"

I grinned at him. "A heap of dynamite."

Mid-afternoon, we camped in the middle of a copse of tall pines. We planned to grab a few hours of sleep for I reckoned the night would be mighty long.

Chapter Sixteen

Leading the packhorse, we topped a hill on the north road overlooking Crockett just before midnight. The night was crisp, and the stars lit the countryside with a bluish silver glow. Pulling up behind a stand of pine, we studied the town. The only lights came from Roche's Saloon. Half a dozen horses stood hipshot at the hitching rail. "Best we leave our horses here and go in on foot," I whispered, my breath frosty in the night.

Speck's voice was shaky. "I don't cotton to breaking into Roche's store. What if some jasper comes out of the saloon and spots us? We'll have the whole town on our necks."

I dismounted. "You worry too much. Let's go."

Moving quickly, I sprinted across a small clearing and ducked into the shadows of the post office. I couldn't help wondering just what had taken place with Sheriff Swain's letter.

"Now what?" Speck whispered as he came up to me.

"Around the back, and stay in the shadows."

Like ghosts, we eased along the back of the post office and the Wells Fargo office, First Texas Bank, the milliners, and finally, Roche's General Store. "Here we are," I whispered, squinting into the night, searching for a window through which we could slip. I spotted one next to the door.

"Hurry up," Speck muttered. "Someone might come by."

"Come on." I eased the window up and climbed inside. Just as Speck threw a leg over the windowsill, a mongrel raced toward him, yapping its head off.

He fell inside, and I hurriedly closed the window, but the dog continued to bark.

"That mutt's going to wake the whole town," he muttered.

A few moments later, a distant shout silenced the dog.

Speck sighed in relief.

We sat without moving for a few minutes, hoping the dog had drifted back into the night. Finally, I lowered the shade, cutting off the starlight and plunging the room into absolute darkness. I struck a match and cupped it in my hands. "You look along that wall for the dynamite and fuses. I'll look over here."

All I found were barrels of flour and slabs of salted bacon.

"Here it is," Speck whispered, his voice trembling with excitement. "Fuses too."

I shoved several coils of fuse into the pockets of my Mackinaw. "Grab a case of dynamite, and let's get out of here."

"Sure hope that mutt ain't out there," he growled as he hoisted a wooden case with three black X's on each side.

"Hold on a minute," I whispered, striking another match and hurrying over to the salted bacon from which I sliced off a slab.

Speck grinned when I held up the bacon. "This'll keep our friend busy."

Easing the back door open, I searched the shadows for the dog. Off to the right came a threatening snarl. I tossed the bacon in the direction of the growl. The growls ceased and moments later I saw a shadow racing into the night. "Now," I whispered over my shoulder, throwing the door wide open.

"What about the door? We can't lock it back."

"Don't worry. The clerk will probably figure he forgot to lock it."

After lashing the dynamite to the packhorse, we eased around the outskirts of town to a spot where we could watch the saloon. The tinny strains of "Sweet Betsy from Pike" drifted through the crisp air. We sat shivering in our saddles, our eyes on the batwing doors of the saloon.

Thirty minutes later, Speck spoke up, his voice mocking. "I'm beginning to wonder if them boys plan on spending the night there."

"I hope not," I replied wryly.

Suddenly, the doors swung open, and two cowpokes stumbled out onto the torch-lit porch. George Millikin was one of them. The other had his arm in a sling. "Who's that with Millikin, the one with the busted arm?"

"Joe Beckner. He must've been the one the sheriff told us about. Hey," Speck exclaimed. "Would you look at that. Ain't that Otsie Bets coming out?"

My eyes narrowed as I watched Otsie stagger out on the porch. A slow grin spread over my face. Without taking my eyes off him, I muttered to Speck, "Let's start with Otsie, Speck. What do you think?"

He chuckled. "I can't think of nothing I'd like better."

Somehow, the drunken cowpoke managed to grab the reins and haul himself into his saddle where his chin slumped to his chest. Dutifully, his pony ambled down the street, taking his unconscious master home.

We followed at a distance. A mile or so south of town, the horse pulled up beside a shack on the side of the road. A pole corral was built next to the house. A privy sat out back.

"Now what?"

Off to the right loomed the dark silhouette of a hill covered with pines. I grinned. "We wait on top of that hill over there, and then here's what we'll do."

After Speck heard what I had in mind, he shook his head slowly. "Blast it, Davy, you're a devious gent."

Slowly, the sky to the east reddened with the rising sun. I climbed to my feet and stretched the kinks from my chilled and cramped muscles, anxious to greet the warm rays of the morning sun. Below, Otsie's house was silent.

Speck yawned. "He up yet?"

"Anytime. You know what to do?"

He chuckled. "I can't wait. I just wish he was inside when it goes up."

"Let's ease on down."

"I just thought of something," Speck muttered, nodding to the board in my hand. "What if Otsie can't read?"

I looked at the board I had taken from one of the dynamite cases. On it I had written the warning, *Next time, the house goes with you in it,* in charcoal. "Then for his own good, I'd hope he'd take it to somebody who could read."

"What if he don't?"

"Bad luck for him," I replied with a crooked grin.

We separated. I headed for the front of the house and crouched by the corner. Speck hid in the bushes behind the privy. I heard stirring inside through the board and batten walls. Moments later, the back door creaked open. As soon as I heard the privy door shut, I hurried through the front door and propped the warning against the coffee pot sitting on the potbellied stove. And then I scooted back through the trees to our camp.

Below, the privy door opened, and Otsie shuffled back to his shack. At the same time, Speck tossed the stick of dynamite on the ground at the rear of the privy. The fuse was long enough that he could get beyond the range of the falling debris.

At that moment, Otsie came out the front of the house holding the warning. He looked around, scratched his head, and went back inside. Seconds later, he appeared at the rear door, searching for who-ever had left him the note.

That's when the privy exploded, the concussion knocking Otsie back into the house.

"If he's still here tonight, we'll do the house." I grinned at Speck. "Now, what do you say we find us some deep woods and take us a nap?"

"Coffee too?"

"And coffee too."

Just as we climbed onto our ponies, we spotted Otsie racing for town, the board clutched in his hand. "Hold on," I said. "Let's see what's going to happen."

The small copse of pine from which we observed Otsie Bets' shack blanketed the crest of a hill rising thirty or forty feet above the surrounding terrain. In addition to having a clear view of the town to the north, we could see miles in all directions, which provided us ample time to seek other shelter in case unwanted riders approached.

Fifteen minutes later, two riders rode out of town in our direction. We watched as they approached. I recognized Otsie by the sorrel he forked, and finally recognized our ex-cowpuncher, John Bratton, as the two reined up at the shack.

"What do you think?" Speck whispered.

I shook my head, keeping my eyes on the shack. A few minutes later, Bratton emerged from the cabin, walked around it studying the surrounding hills, then climbed onto his horse and headed back to Crockett.

Moments later, Otsie stepped outside and peered after Bratton. When Bratton was out of sight, the diminutive cowpoke rushed back inside and reappeared with saddlebags and a bedroll. He fumbled to lash his gear behind the cantle and without a backward glance, raced to the south.

Speck grinned at me. "That's one. Who's next?"

"How about Bratton?"

Speck's grin grew wider.

Swamping the saloon for his board and found, Bratton had spread his bedroll on the floor of the saloon's storeroom.

Speck shoved his hat to the back of his head to scratch it. "How are we going to get to him if he's sawing logs in the back room of the saloon?"

"I'll slip in after he goes to sleep and roust him out. We'll give him a horse and escort him out of town."

With a frown, Speck grunted, "What if he won't go? All he's got to do is shout."

I gave Speck an amused grin. "Not with a burning stick of dynamite shoved under his belt."

His eyes grew wide.

"Well," I explained, "he'll *think* it's a stick of dynamite."

Speck furrowed his brows.

"We'll cut a tree limb the size of a stick and fasten a fuse to it. In the dark, he won't know the difference. All he'll see is a burning fuse."

Chapter Seventeen

I've always been amazed at how the best-laid plans can go askew at the last minute. And that's what happened when I went in for Bratton. Everything went out of kilter.

Just outside the back door of the storeroom, I touched a match to the fuse and stepped inside. I jerked to a halt. In the dim light cast by the burning match, I saw that Bratton's bedroll was empty.

Muttering a curse, I turned to leave. At that moment, the door opened and light from a lantern illumined the room. A guttural voice shouted, "Hey, what are you doing in here?"

I didn't know what else to do, so I tossed him the branch with the burning fuse. "Catch," I shouted as I leaped for the door.

Shouts followed us as we raced from town. A mile or so to the west, we pulled into a mixed patch of oak and pine.

I fumbled in my saddlebags and retrieved two sticks of dynamite and handed them to Speck. "Stick fuses in a couple sticks. I'll do the same. We'll give our friends a welcome they won't forget."

Speck chuckled. "Davy, I said it once, and I'll say it again—you ain't a nice man."

"Thanks, Speck. Mighty decent of you to say so."

We both laughed and rigged our dynamite.

Soon, the rumbling of hoof beats rolled through the chilly night. Within a minute or so, the posse galloped around a bend in the road. We waited just inside a stand of pine and oak so thick we were hidden from the view of the riders thundering down the muddy road less than thirty feet from us.

I held a match near the tips of the two fuses, my thumbnail on the head. "You ready?"

He chuckled. "You bet."

The shadowed forms of the posse raced toward us. When they drew within thirty yards, I whispered harshly, "Now! Light 'em and throw 'em."

I scratched my nail on the match head. Nothing. I shot a hasty glance at the approaching riders and tried again. This time, the match flared. I cupped it in my hand to hide the light from the eyes of the posse, although I knew they would quickly spot the burning fuses in the darkness. By the time they saw the fuses and recognized them for what they were, it would be too late.

The tips of the two fuses flared when I touched them to the match flame. My bay jittered about, alarmed at the sudden hissing light behind its head.

Rearing back, I threw the first one as far as I could into the night. It arced through the air, leaving behind a rainbow of yellow sparks. Even before the first one reached its apex, I tossed the second.

From the corner of my eye, I saw Speck's first stick arc through the air. The first stick exploded, sending the posse in all directions. To my horror, Speck's second toss slammed into a tree trunk and bounced back toward us.

We couldn't turn back into the stand of pine and oak. They grew too thick for us to get beyond the range of the dynamite before it exploded. Our only chance was forward, right into the maw of the posse, which by now was a melee of confusion. I dug my spurs into the bay, and the frightened animal leaped from the timber. Speck was right behind me.

Then came a second explosion followed almost instantly by a third as we sped through the shadows of rearing horses and cursing men. A fourth explosion followed, and moments later, a tree crashed to the ground.

I expected pursuit, but hearing none after a few minutes, I pulled off the road and dropped my pony into a trot.

Speck pulled up beside me. "Whew," he whistled through his lips.

"A word of warning, Partner. Don't you never go entering any dynamite throwing contest. And if you do, let me know so I can be somewhere else."

He laughed softly. "Thing just slipped out of my hand. Now what? Find someplace for the night?"

"Not yet. We've got another job before we call it a night."

"What's that?"

"Our friends back there. When they get back to town, they'll report to Roche. I think maybe we should give our own report to Roche."

In the pale starlight, I saw a knowing grin split across Speck's angular face.

We were sitting in our saddles in the shadows between the saloon and the general store when four riders turned onto the main street from the west road.

I pulled out two sticks and waited. "When they dismount we'll ride into the street, throw the sticks, and hightail it out of here."

Speck chuckled. "I'm right behind you."

As soon as the riders moved out of sight past the corner of the general store, I touched a match to my fuses. Sparks flew. "You ready?"

Speck whispered back. "Yep."

I sent my bay racing into the street and turned him

north. As we shot past the riders dismounting in front of the bank, we lobbed our dynamite at them.

A cacophony of sharp curses, terrifying screams, and squealing horses filled the night, all suddenly drowned by four almost instantaneous explosions.

Overhead, clouds moved across the sky, hiding the stars. "We'd best find us a dark spot to hunker down in. It's going to be blacker than a blacksmith's apron in a few minutes," I shouted as we raced to the north.

The pounding of hooves awakened us the next morning. Easing toward the edge of the timber on foot, I peered across the prairies. A dozen riders bundled against the cold were thundering along the north road. Sliding behind a large pine, I watched as they passed and disappeared from sight up the road. I started to turn back to our cold camp when I froze.

A single rider had returned, studying the sides of the road. When he was directly in front of me, he stared at the road intently, then lifted his gaze to the woods in which we had hidden. I pressed up against the thick pine. My pulse grew faster.

I heard him click his tongue to send his pony ambling toward us. He continued to study the ground, and grew closer. He was a stranger to me, but he must have been a fairly keen observer to pick up our sign.

Slowly, I slid my Colt from the holster.

By now, he was within a few feet of the timber, less

than fifteen or so from me. He squinted, trying to penetrate the shadows of the stand.

Taking a deep breath, I stepped out where he could see me and cocked my Colt. "Make a move, Cowboy, and it'll be your last. And don't put up your hands."

He froze. I took a few steps toward him.

His eyes shifted nervously.

"Do what I say, and you'll live through this. Buck me, and you'll find yourself trying to figure out whether you want the comfort of heaven or the company of Hades. You understand?"

He nodded.

"Good. Now, climb down off that pony."

"You ain't gettin' away with this," he growled.

"Looks to me like I am, Partner." I jerked the muzzle of my Colt sharply toward the ground. "Now git, or I'll help you git."

Glaring at me, he climbed down.

I sat him next to a pine and tied him nice and snug. Then I tied his legs stretched wide. Just as I finished, Speck came up, his face tight with alarm. "Who's that?"

"One of Fain's posse."

Speck scanned the trees about us hastily. "Where are the others?"

"Up the road." With my eyes fixed on the hogtied cowboy, I spoke to Speck. "Bring me a stick of dynamite."

The cowboy's eyes grew wide. Unable to suppress the trembling in his voice, he asked, "What are you going to do?"

"Make certain Fain and jaspers like you know you're playing with the big boys now."

"Here you are, Davy," Speck said, handing me a fused stick of dynamite.

I knelt and very deliberately worked the stick into the ground between his spread legs.

His eyes narrowed. "That don't scare me none."

I winked at Speck. "Lookee here. We got us a brave one."

"Yeah."

"Yeah," he growled. "Fain ain't going to like you roughing up any of his boys.

"Now, friend, that really bothers me." Striking a match, I touched it to the fuse, then backed away and lazily pulled out my Bull Durham and began rolling a cigarette.

The hogtied cowpoke gasped and looked up at me in horror. "You crazy?"

Before he could continue, I nodded, at the same time, sticking the freshly built cigarette between my lips and fumbling for a match. "Major fault in my character I've been told." I gestured to Speck. "Best back away behind one of those trees. Going to be mighty messy around here in a few seconds." I took a drag off the cigarette, at the same time casting a quick glance at the fuse. "Shame some jaspers got to be so stubborn."

When the cowpoke saw Speck back away and hide behind a tree, he started blubbering. All the bravado, the bluster swept away on the winds of fear. His eyes bulged as he stared down at the burning fuse between his spread legs.

When he clamped his eyes shut in anticipation of the explosion, I yanked the fuse from the dynamite and tossed it on the ground.

Moments later, when the hissing died away, he opened his eyes slowly.

"Not this time, Cowboy. But, I catch you riding with this posse again—" I tapped the dynamite slowly. "You figure it out."

We headed west, staying in the timber. I was tired, and from the dark circles under Speck's eyes, he was worn to a frazzle just like me.

The lanky cowpoke cleared his throat. "You reckon we're doing any good, Davy?"

I pondered the question. "I don't know, Speck. I truly don't know. Otsie's gone, and who can say about that jasper back there. I don't have any inkling about the others." I paused and looked at him, a risky suggestion on the tip of my tongue. "But, maybe we ought to find out."

He frowned. "And how do you reckon we do that? Just walk up and ask Roche?"

"Not a bad idea, except instead of Roche, we'll go to Lum Bishop tonight."

"Bishop? The old boy at the post office?"

"Who else would have a better handle on town matters?"

He eyed me doubtfully. "That means going back into town."

"Me. You stay out with the horses."

"But you need a lookout," he protested.

"We need the horses more."

He drew a deep breath and blew out through his lips. "I sure got a bad feeling about tonight, Davy. Feels like somebody done walked over my grave."

I laughed, but the truth was, I had the same feeling.

Chapter Eighteen

Leaving our packhorse and dynamite in our camp, we headed for town. Well after dark, we reined up in a stand of pines a short distance from town. Lum Bishop lived in a room behind the post office, which was the last building on the east side of the main street.

Dismounting, I picked my way through the timber around to the rear of his living quarters. After peering left and right into the darkness, I sprinted from the trees into the shadows of the post office and knocked on the back door. Moments later, the yellow glow of a coal oil lamp shone out the window, laying a panel of yellow on the muddy ground. The door opened a crack and Bishop peered out. "Who's out there?"

I whispered urgently, "It's me, Lum. Davy Nelson."

"Nelson?" He jerked the door open. "Get your carcass in here. Quick."

I darted inside, and he slammed the door behind me. "What the Sam Hill are you doing here?" he demanded, jerking the window shade down.

"You're the only one I can trust, Lum. I don't reckon we got an answer to the sheriff's letter yet."

He ran his hand over his bald head. "Not yet, and you know, Davy, there ain't no assurance we'll even get one."

I muttered a curse. "You know what Speck and me have been doing?"

Grinning up at me, he replied with a chuckle. "Who don't? Roche is fit to be tied. He's already had two or three men just up and leave town, but he just hires more to replace them." He glanced at the window. "Where's Speck? Where you boys been staying?"

"Wherever we can. Speck's holding the horses out in the timber."

"You been back to the Bar M?"

I shook my head.

The small man continued. "Roche put a couple gunnies out there when he learned you all had deserted it."

I chuckled. "I figured that. Who?"

"Millikin and Beckner."

"Millikin, huh?" I remembered him from my first day in Crockett. "Well, I got me a feeling those two jaspers will sure regret staying out there."

Lum Bishop frowned. "What are—" He waved his

hand. "Forget it. I don't know what you have in mind, and I don't want to know."

"What do the others in town think? You reckon there are any we could depend on to help?"

The small man thought a moment. "Well, there's been a heap of excited talk about it. Several of them, like Hank Warner down at the livery and Lester Potts at the blacksmith shop—or what's left of the blacksmith shop," he added with a wry grin.

"But, they work for Roche."

With a shrug, Bishop replied, "Most of the town works for him but that don't mean they care for him. Yes, sir, I'd say if the right situation arose, you could get some help from them."

"Well then, do me a favor. Keep your ears open for whoever we might be able to call on just in case that right situation comes around."

He grinned. "Count on it."

A sharp knock at the door startled us. I jerked around as a voice called out. "Lum. Lum Bishop. This is the sheriff. Are you all right? Let me in."

Lum pointed to the door leading to the post office. "That way. Hurry. Go out the front and come around the side. I'll send Fain out the front."

I turned to leave, but he stopped me. "Wait. How do I get in touch with you?"

"Head out the west road. I'll find you."

He nodded, and I slipped into the post office and out the front door and around the side, ducking into the shadows just outside Lum Bishop's living quarters. I grinned when I heard the little man exclaim. "Am I glad to see you, Sheriff. Davy Nelson was here. He wanted money to get out of town. He ran out through the front."

As the sound of running feet vanished into the post office, I turned back to the horses. Suddenly, I froze, glimpsing movement ahead of me. I dropped into a crouch, and backtracked past the post office. When I reached the Wells Fargo depot, I paused, hearing voices coming toward me.

Moving as quietly as I could, I darted past the general store and paused once again, this time outside the back door to the saloon. My blood ran cold when I heard voices ahead of me. I was trapped!

I pressed up against the clapboard walls of the saloon. The voices on either side drew nearer. I stretched my arm to the left, searching for the back door. My fingers touched the knob. Holding my breath, I turned it and gently pushed. The door swung open.

I had no idea what I was stepping into, but it couldn't be any worse than what I was facing out here. The voices grew louder.

"I'd sure like to get that Nelson in my sights," one said.

"Me too," a second responded. "I could use the five hundred Roche put on his head.

Tiptoeing up the steps, I slipped into the darkened storeroom and eased the door shut.

"What was that?" one of the voices exclaimed.

"What? I didn't hear nothing."

Several seconds of silence passed. "Reckon it was my imagination. Come on. Let's go get us a drink. Fain said Roche has some orders for us."

My ears perked up. Roche. Orders. I looked into the darkness in the direction of the rear door. If I waited a few minutes until Roche's men drifted into the saloon, I could escape. On the other hand, here was a chance to maybe get a leg up on Carl Roche. Find out what he had in mind.

I knew I was taking a chance by going deeper into the lion's den—the weasel's in this case—but I figured it was worth the risk.

Feeling my way through the dark, I found a door. I opened it a crack and peered out. To my left was the fancy bar, running the entire length of the wall. Glancing up, I saw a stairway above me. To my right, backed up against the base of the stairway sat a battered piano, providing a dark little cave under the stairs.

Directly in front of me was another bar, this one not in use. It stretched along the wall to the piano.

Roche and half a dozen cowpokes were seated around a table near the piano. Dropping to my hands and knees, I crawled along the bar to the piano and ducked into the tiny cubicle under the stairs.

I could hear Roche plainly. I grinned to myself as I looked around my little cubbyhole. I was nice and snug. When Roche left, all I had to do was stay put until the bartender closed up, and then hightail it back to where Speck was waiting.

"Where's Cooter?" Roche demanded.

"On his way, Mister Roche. Look. There he is."

"You took your own good time, Cooter." Roche's tone was hard and critical.

"Nelson was in town," the new sheriff announced.

"Nelson! Did you get him?" Roche demanded.

"Never saw hide or hair of him, Mister Roche. I saw the light on in Lum Bishop's place. When I knocked, Nelson ran out the front."

"What was he doing at Lum's place?"

"Trying to get enough money to get out of town."

Roche cursed. "We've got to put a stop to his meddling. I lost three men today. I don't know if Nelson killed them or they just run off. I got Millikin and Beckner at the Bar M. I've half a mind to send Bratton out there too."

Cooter Fain whined. "Nelson and Speck is like ghosts. You glimpse them, and then they're gone."

Roche snorted. "They won't be like ghosts any longer. I hired me a top-notch tracker, Johnny Two-Shoes. Part Cherokee, part Comanche."

"Is he good?"

"From what I'm paying him, he'd better be."

"Hey, what are you doing there?" I jerked around at

the exclamation. The bartender stood staring at me, just as surprised as I was.

With a wild shout, I leaped to my feet and threw my shoulder into the piano, shoving it across the floor and into Roche's table, sending Roche and his owlhoots sprawling on the sawdust-covered floor.

I couldn't go forward. I couldn't go back. So I bounded up the stairs, staying low. My bad leg gave way and I stumbled, falling flat on the stairs, but I sprang to my feet instantly. Dragging my right leg, I was halfway up when the first six-gun roared and a chunk of wood exploded from the rail just in front of me. Several more followed, humming like bees.

Below, Roche waved frantically and screamed. "Get him! Get him! Get him!"

At the top of the stairs, I raced down the hall. Behind me, boots pounded up the wooden treads. I slammed open a door and hobbled into a room, hoping I'd picked one with a balcony. When the light from the open door spilled across the bed, two figures sat up abruptly. The hirsute man started cursing, and the young woman started screaming, at the same time yanking the covers up about her neck. Without slowing, I touched my fingers to the tip of my Stetson. "Sorry, folks. Just passing through. Don't let me disturb you."

I threw open the door to the balcony and stepped out. The shouts behind me grew closer. I glanced at the ground, which appeared to be a mighty long way down, much farther than the roof of Roche's General Store next door. That was it. Jump to the roof, slide down, then drop the last eight or ten feet to the ground.

And by the time Roche's men clambered back down the stairs, Speck and me would be racing into the night. I climbed over the rail and jumped.

I braced myself for the impact but to my horror I went right through the roof, collapsing a portion of it to the floor below. I slammed into a barrel of flour, which exploded and filled the room with a choking white dust.

Like a bull I stumbled and stormed through the merchandise to the storeroom, coughing and gasping from the flour. When I jerked the back door open, a jasper stood there with a lantern. His eyes bulged when he spotted me all covered with flour.

"What the—"

He didn't have time to finish his exclamation for I kicked him in the forehead.

I raced through the darkness.

Behind me, the night echoed with reports of six-guns and angry shouts from Roche and his men.

When Speck saw me approaching, he said, "I was beginning to get worried about—" He stopped in mid-sentence when he saw that I was white all over. "What the blazes?"

"I'll tell you later," I said, swinging into my saddle. "Let's ride. There's a heap of angry gents back there."

Chapter Nineteen

Roche's boys moved faster than I expected. Just as we burst from the timber onto the north road, several cowpokes pulled away from the hitching rail and raced after us.

"I reckon you've stirred yourself up a hornet's nest," Speck shouted above the pounding of our horses' hooves.

The stars bathed the road in a bluish silver light. Keeping my eyes on the side of the road ahead, I fumbled for one of the ropes I carried and shook out a loop.

"What—"

Before Speck could finish his question, I spotted what I had been looking for—a broken limb projecting from an oak. "Keep going," I shouted, at the same time slowing my bay and tossing the loop over the limb. Quickly, I stretched it across the road head high and dallied it around the trunk tightly before knotting it with two fast half-hitches.

Digging my spurs into the bay, I raced after Speck who was waiting nervously for me to catch up.

The pounding hooves grew closer.

Suddenly, a piercing scream split the cold night air followed by the startled squeals of a horse.

The chill in the air numbed my cheeks. We rode hard for the next twenty minutes before angling off the road and racing between two stands of timber and into a series of tree-covered ridges that rose a hundred feet or so above the rolling countryside.

Earlier in the day, on the far side of the third ridge, we had discovered a windfall that had settled over a gulch cut by running water—one deep enough to hide us and the horses.

At a bend in the gully, the water had cut underneath the bank, offering a spot for a fire that could not be seen from outside. The heat reflected off the red clay bank, providing a warm and snug refuge against the chill beyond.

I brushed off what flour I could and rolled out my bedroll, grateful for the chance to rest my leg. I was exhausted. That and the fact that we were warm and snug almost put us in Roche's hands.

Voices awakened me early next morning. I jerked

upright and scrambled from my blankets, grabbing my Winchester and poking my head above the windfall. I grimaced when I put weight on my lame leg. Like the doc had said, cold weather wasn't a friend to my leg.

"What do you see?" Speck whispered from inside.

"Nothing, yet."

I studied the ridge in front of me. Nothing was moving. Then I heard the voices again, back behind me. Pivoting, I scanned the ridge above. Still nothing. Moving slowly, I crawled from our cubbyhole and eased upward, dropping to my belly as I drew near the crest of the ridge.

Removing my hat, I peered over the top. On the far ridge to the east, six riders were strung out in a single line, tagging after their leader, an Indian astride a paint pony.

Every sense became alert. I remembered Roche's words from the night before. He had hired a tracker, a Cherokee-Comanche by the name of Johnny Two-Shoes. I squinted into the early morning light at the lanky rider wearing a black slouch hat. That had to be him.

For the first time, I noticed the sky was overcast with ominous gray clouds. Scooting back down to our camp, I grabbed my gear. "Let's hustle. We'll have unwelcome guests in about thirty minutes."

"Roche's boys?"

I nodded. "And with a tracker. Hurry it up," I added, giving a final tug on the cinch. "We've got to put as much distance between us and them as we can."

Clucking his tongue, Speck swung into his saddle. "Sure wish we had us some more of that dynamite we left back at the old camp."

"You know what they say about hindsight."

"Yep. Reckon I do."

I led out, heading to the bottom of the ridge and turning south, deliberately riding into a tangle of undergrowth that I hoped would delay our pursuers.

At the south end of the ridge, we cut west, heading for Trinity River. The wind freshened, carrying with it an icy chill. I prayed for rain; if not rain, then snow, anything to cover our sign, which stood out in the muddy ground like a crib girl at a Ladies' Temperance social.

Twenty minutes later, we left the ridge behind, sprinting across a rolling prairie to a stand of pine a mile or so away.

Once inside the protection of the pines, we pulled up to give our ponies a rest. "Think we shook them?"

"Nope." I shook my head. "Ground's too soft. They can follow us across the prairie at a gallop with the sign we left."

"Maybe not," Speck replied, a grin playing over this thin lips. "Look yonder." He pointed through the trees. "That give you any ideas?"

I smiled when I spotted the small herd of grazing horses. "Reckon it does."

He popped the reins on his horse's neck. "Let's get it going."

We raced from the timber and put the grazing horses on the run. We stayed on either side, trying to steer the spooked ponies toward the river.

They flew like the wind, ears back, eyes rolling, teeth bared, manes flying, and we flew right with them. We rode hard and finally hit the flood plain. The churning, boiling Trinity River cut through the flatland less than a mile ahead.

Our trail was so plain that even a blind man could follow it. We veered the herd to the left, in the direction of what appeared to be a gully cut by water running off the plain to the river.

"Drive them all in," I shouted, then swim downriver and climb out on the other side."

Speck shook his head. Through clenched teeth, he shouted above the thunder of hooves. "Blast it, Davy. You're always trying to make me go swimming."

"You got a better idea?"

He shook his head. "Reckon not."

The herd slowed as we approached the gully. They paused at the rim, feet together, then, pushing off with their hind feet, leaped down into the gully. Moments later, we hit the icy waters of the river right behind the herd.

Letting the current push us, we swam downriver for a half-mile or so as one after the other, the animals clambered from the river and headed off in different directions.

"Over there," Speck shouted, indicating a shallow gully that led to the west bank.

Minutes later, we stood back in the shelter of a copse of willow and oak, studying our back trail, our teeth chattering from the cold.

The wind picked up and with it, a few splatters of chilling rain. I shivered and grimaced against the throbbing in my leg.

"There they are," Speck whispered harshly.

A mile or so to the north, I spotted six riders crossing the flood plain. They followed the trail to the gully, then headed downriver.

I dismounted and pinched my bay's nostrils to keep him from whinnying if he caught the scent of the other horses. Speck did the same.

The wind intensified, cutting through my soaked clothes and driving chills to the marrow of my bones. I hunkered down in my Mackinaw, grateful for the wool coat, which though wet, still provided warmth. My legs felt like ice.

Across the river, the riders paused, pointing out tracks along the way. There were so many tracks going so many different ways that finally, Johnny Two-Shoes turned and spoke to the rider behind him.

I squinted, trying to make out the second jasper's features.

"That looks like Cooter to me," Speck muttered.

"Think so?" I couldn't make him out.

"Bet a dollar on it."

At that moment, Cooter stared at the river, then wheeled his horse about, waving his arm to signal that they were returning to town.

Even after they disappeared into the woods beyond the flood plain, we watched. Finally, I said, "You know where we are?"

"Yep." He pointed southeast. "Bar M's about ten miles thataway."

"I don't know about you, but I wouldn't mind paying it a visit. See if Roche's boys are taking care of the place for us."

Speck looked around at me, a wry grin on his lips. "They probably are, but I'm with you—might as well take a look."

"Tell you what," I replied, climbing stiffly back into the saddle. "Let's ride downriver in these woods a few miles before we cross. Then we can build a fire and dry out."

Speck cut his eyes to the trees into which the search party had disappeared beyond the plain. "Reckon you're right, Davy. Reckon you're right." He paused, then added ruefully. "I'd sure hate to have to cross that river again."

As long as we remained in the trees, we had some protection from the biting wind and icy rain, but when we dropped down to the river, we caught the full brunt of the coming storm.

Grimly, we drove our horses into the river, clambering out on the far side a few minutes later and scrambling up the steep bank to the protection of the trees where we built a fire.

Once we figured we were reasonably dry, we headed south, staying in the trees until Speck opined we were due west of the Bar M. "Let's ride another mile or so," I said.

"Huh?"

"I'd feel better coming into the ranch from the rear. If Roche still has Beckner and Millikin out there, I reckon they'll be in the main house. If we come in from the back, we'll have the ranch buildings between us and the house."

"That there fire back yonder didn't help too much. I'm going to be nothing but icicles when we get there, I reckon," he muttered, his teeth chattering.

"At least we'll be live icicles."

Chapter Twenty

Night came early, and the threatening storm had not broken by the time we reined up in a motte of pine on a hill overlooking the ranch. Lights shone from the windows of the main house and smoke poured from the chimney, but was quickly blown away by the chilling wind.

Dropping down to the ranch, we slipped into corral behind the barn and led the horses inside. It was so black the bats probably stayed home. The ponies in the barn whinnied when they scented our mounts.

"Blast," Speck muttered.

"Easy, boy," I whispered, patting my bay on the neck. "Easy."

I felt for a stall rail and looped the reins around it.

"Look!" The urgency in Speck's tone alerted me. "Someone's coming."

I peered through a crack in the boards. A dark figure strode toward the barn, a lantern swinging back and forth in the darkness. He was muttering curses. The light from the lantern revealed the scowling face of George Millikin.

"Duck," I whispered, pressing up against the wall next to the door.

Moments later, the door creaked open. Snow gusted inside, swirling around Millikin. I stepped forward, jabbing the muzzle of my revolver in the middle of his back. "Hold it right there, Millikin. Don't move a step."

He stiffened. "Who—"

At that moment, Speck stepped from the shadows of the stall in which he had been hiding.

Millikin gasped. "Speck Webster!"

"Howdy, Millikin," the lanky cowpoke replied, lazily pointing his six-gun at the startled owlhoot's belly.

"Now," I said, my voice cold. "You're going to do exactly what I say. You understand?" I jabbed the muzzle hard into his back. He winced. "I asked if you understand?"

He nodded jerkily and croaked, "Yeah. I understand."

"Who's in there with you?"

"Beckner. Joe Beckner."

"Anyone else?"

"No." He shook his head.

I poked him again. "You'd better not be lying to me. If I see anyone else, I'll blow a hole in your back."

Millikin hesitated, his pudgy face crumbling. "All right, all right. Bratton's in there too. John Bratton."

Speck and I exchanged knowing smiles.

Slipping his six-gun from his holster and tucking it under my belt, I growled, "Now listen to me. You're going to march back to the house with us behind you. If you mutter any kind of warning, you'll be the first to hit the floor. Understand?"

The big-bellied cowpoke nodded.

"Grab some rope, Speck." I poked Millikin again. "Now, git."

Engrossed in their poker game, neither Bratton nor Beckner looked up from their cards when we entered. The latter cowboy growled over his shoulder. "Find out what was spooking the horses?"

"Sure did, boys," I said. "Me."

At the sound of my voice, they leaped to their feet, grabbing at their six-guns. "Don't try it," I shouted.

Beckner froze, but Bratton cursed and slapped leather. My Colt roared twice, punching holes in his chest. He froze, his six-gun pointed at the floor. The big man looked at me in disbelief. A trickle of blood ran down the side of his lips. His legs wobbled slightly, then gave way, and he fell face forward to the floor.

Both Beckner and Millikin gaped at me in stunned surprise. With a cold smile, I swung the muzzle of my

Colt on them. Millikin's eyes grew wide in alarm. "Hold on, Nelson. I ain't drawing. You wouldn't kill someone in cold blood."

I eyed the two of them. "You two, I could. Now, turn around, both of you, and put your hands behind you."

Beckner eyed me defiantly. "I got a busted arm."

"Put your good hand behind you then, or take the same trip Bratton took."

Reluctantly, the grizzled cowpoke stuck his hand behind him.

"Tie his hand to his busted arm, Speck. Don't reckon he'll jerk too hard on it."

With a chuckle, Speck tied both jaspers tight. "Now, sit," I ordered, nodding in the direction of some chairs.

After they sat, I studied them for several seconds. "I'm not sure what to do with you two." I nodded to the motionless body of John Bratton. "At least, you weren't stupid enough to try what he tried." I picked up a rope and slowly built a hangman's knot, from time to time glancing at each of them.

"Maybe I should just hang you two." I gestured to the heavy roof joists above. "We could hang them right here, Speck," I said, keeping my eyes on the two cowpokes.

Beckner glared at me, his close-set eyes seething with hate.

Millikin's breathing grew rapid. His Adam's apple bobbed.

I tossed the rope to Speck. "Build me another one, Speck. I need two."

He grinned and quickly built another hangman's loop while I stepped behind the two cowpokes and blindfolded them. Beckner tried to move his head, but I jerked it back and snugged down the blindfold.

Millikin whined, "Don't, Nelson. I beg you. I'll do anything you say."

Beckner growled, "Shut up, Millikin."

"I don't want to die," he cried.

"He ain't going to do nothing. He's just bluffing."

For a moment, Millikin stopped sobbing, but when I dropped the hangman's loop over his head, he bawled like a baby.

Beckner stiffened when he felt the loop tighten about his neck. "You ain't got the guts, Nelson. I—"

I yanked on the rope, cutting off his protests. "Shut up and stand up." He choked and gasped, but he did as I said. "Now, climb up in that chair."

He hesitated. I jabbed my revolver in his belly. "Climb up in the chair or eat a lead plum." I winked at Speck. "Give this old boy a hand, Speck. Wouldn't want him to fall and hurt himself."

Next, we helped Millikin onto his chair while he continued to blubber.

"All right, Speck, toss your rope over the beam."

We threw the ropes over the beam and tugged them tight. I winked at him. "Tie the end to those other beams. They look strong enough to hold these two." I handed him a piece of firewood, which would keep the rope taut, but easily be jerked off the floor if either fell from his chair.

Speck slapped his hands together briskly when he finished. "There, we got it done. How about something to eat while we wait for the fun, Davy?"

"Let's us haul Bratton outside first. Staring at a dead man doesn't do much for my appetite.

We carried Bratton out onto the porch and wrapped him in canvas.

Back inside, I removed my wet Mackinaw and draped it over a straight-back chair by the fire to dry while Speck sliced strips from a slab of salted pork and popped them in the skillet.

Millikin continued to sob, but Beckner remained silent.

Speck poured us some coffee and plopped down at the table. "Bad thing about this, Davy, is if we hang them, we got to bury them. And the ground is mighty hard out there." He winked at me.

I grinned. "No need to bury them. Stack them like cordwood out behind the corral with Bratton. The critters'll take care of them for us."

Millikin babbled, "Please, Nelson. Don't do it. I—" He broke into sobs again, dropping his head to his chest.

I took a sip of coffee. "Well, there might be a chance for you two."

"What? Anything. Anything," Millikin blubbered.

"Who shot Ed McCall?"

"Shut your mouth, Millikin." Beckner warned.

The frightened cowboy gulped hard. "If—if I tell you, will you let me go?"

Speck chuckled. "In case you ain't noticed it, Partner, you ain't in no position to do no bargaining."

"He's right, Millikin. Now, who did it?"

"I told you to keep your mouth shut," Beckner screamed.

I barked at Beckner. "You keep your mouth shut, or I'll slap a gag on you. Now, who shot him, Millikin?"

"I-I don't know. I—"

"Too bad."

"No, no. I mean, Roche sent Cooter and Beckner out after McCall left the notary. When they came back, Cooter told Roche that McCall was took care of."

"A notary, huh? For the mortgage payment?"

Millikin nodded slowly.

I had suspected as much, but I reminded myself, George Millikin's admission was worthless with Cooter Fain as sheriff.

I winked at Speck. "Well, Boys, Speck and me, we're mighty hungry. Reckon we'll finish up our supper here before we decide what to do with you."

"But-but, you said—" Millikin stammered.

"I said nothing. Besides, there's no law around here except Roche's. What you told us isn't worth a spoonful of beans."

* * *

By the time we finished our supper, the two owl-hoots were growing tired. Beckner kept shifting his weight from one foot to the other, and Millikin's knees buckled slightly several times.

"Careful, Boys. You don't want to fall off those chairs." I nodded for Speck to follow me outside.

On the porch, I told him to saddle their ponies and tie them to the hitching rail in front of the house. "Saddle up an extra horse so we can send Bratton back to town."

He arched an eyebrow. "You letting them go?"

"If I read them right, Millikin will run faster than a church deacon takes up collection. Beckner?" I shook my head briefly. "I'm afraid I'll end up killing him."

Speck returned several minutes later. He nodded as he plopped down at the table. I cleared my throat. In a slow drawl, I said, "Well, boys. I'm mighty tired. I reckon it's about time to put you to sleep also. Speck, you stand behind Beckner's chair. I'll take care of Millikin here. Now, boys, I reckon it's only Christian to give you a choice. You can jump off the chair, or we'll pull them out from under you." I glanced at Speck who was doing his darndest to keep from laughing.

"Nelson! No," Millikin cried. "In the name of the Lord, don't! I told you what you wanted to know."

"Last chance. Jump or else!"

Beckner blurted out just as I nodded to Speck. "I'll see you in—"

We yanked the chairs from under the two.

They both screamed, then hit the floor and sprawled onto their sides.

After a few moments to let the realization that they weren't dead soak into their thick skulls, we hauled them up into a sitting position and removed the blindfolds. They blinked several times before gaping up at me in disbelief. I glared at them coldly. "That was just a warning, boys. Speck has your ponies outside. We're turning you loose. If you're smart, you'll leave town. Next time I see either of you hardcases, I'll shoot you down like a dog. Understand?"

Millikin nodded, but Beckner just glared at me.

Taking my knife from my boot, I slashed Millikin's bonds. "I'm turning you loose first. Beckner here is going to be our guest a few more hours. You got him and Roche after you now as well as me. I don't know how smart you are, but were I you, I'd light out for parts unknown."

He laid his hand on his holster. "I need my six-gun."

Speck laughed. "We may be dumb, but we ain't stupid. I took your saddle gun too."

I jabbed my finger at him. "We're giving you your life. That's all. Now, in three hours, I'm turning Beckner loose. The longer you hang around here arguing, the better your chances of getting yourself shot down."

The big-bellied man glanced at Beckner, then back at us. In one motion, he grabbed his coat and turned to the door. Speck followed him outside, returning moments later. "He's gone. Heading south." He looked at Beckner, then back to me. "Reckon he'll come back?"

I shook my head. "No."

Three hours later, we turned Beckner loose with instructions to take Bratton back to town. He glared at us from astride his horse. "We'll be back for you two, that's a promise."

I laughed. "You're going to have to do better than what you old boys have been doing."

Chapter Twenty-one

Speck held his hands out to the fire and rubbed them together briskly. He shivered. "Sure hate to go back out in that cold."

"Lesser of two evils," I muttered, enjoying the warmth put out by the leaping flames. I glanced at the regulator clock on the mantle. "It's midnight. I'd say we need to be out of here in an hour or so."

With a frown, Speck replied, "But Beckner and Roche's gunhands won't be back for three or four hours."

"I know, but we need time for the snow to cover our tracks. Don't forget that Cherokee-Comanche tracker Roche put onto us."

*   *   *

By three A.M., we were back in our first camp where we rigged canvas flies to break the wind and hide a fire. The thick pines acted as a windbreak. That and the flies provided us as snug a camp as we could expect, but it didn't do a heap toward easing the throbbing in my leg.

Cupping a tin mug of coffee in both hands, Speck huddled down in his Mackinaw and sipped the steaming liquid, looking up at me from under his eyebrows. He had a worried expression on his angular face. "I sure wish I knew what was going on in town. You think we're really doing any good, Davy? Roche has more than enough money to keep hiring hardcases."

All I could do was shrug. "We're doing all we can without blowing up the town."

Speck hesitated and arched an eyebrow.

Shaking my head, I replied, "That's pretty drastic. Think of the town's citizens. I wouldn't want any of them to get hurt."

He snorted. "Maybe that's what they need. Give them enough backbone to stand up to Roche."

I had to admit he was probably right, but that was one thing I wasn't going to count on. "Let's keep an eye on the west road today. Lum Bishop might be riding out. If he doesn't, we'll go in tonight."

"You remember last time we went into town," Speck warned me, a worried expression on his face.

"Yep," I replied. "I remember."

We spent the day observing the west road. The only riders we spotted were three of Roche's hardcases with Cooter Fain in the lead. They were heading back to Crockett, and the sun was setting in the west.

"Wonder how many he sent out to the ranch with Beckner," Speck muttered.

"What I wonder is how many men Roche has left."

Speck arched an eyebrow at me, a guarded expression on his face. With a trace of resignation edging his words, he said, "Well, I reckon we'll find out tonight, huh?"

I grinned at him. "Reckon so."

On the way into town, we put together a simple plan. "If I need help, I'll fire two shots, one right after the other. You toss a stick of dynamite, then bring the horses around to the north side of town where you were the other night. The explosion should draw their attention, give me time to slip out."

Lum Bishop ran his hand over his bald head. "Word on the street is that George Millikin and two other of Roche's men have disappeared. Folks about are wondering if you might have killed them or if they ran."

"How many men do you figure Roche has left?"

A flicker of fear flashed in the diminutive postmaster's eyes. "Maybe a dozen, but he had a new one ride in today. A killer named Broken-Nose Jack."

Having been back east for the last six years, it came as no surprise that I'd never heard of Broken Nose Jack. "A killer, you say?"

"Yep. Down from Fort Worth. Talk has it he's sent over a dozen waddies to Boot Hill."

At that moment, a knock on the rear door startled us. I ducked into the darkened post office. Through the closed door, I heard a disjointed voice tell Lum to remain inside. "The sheriff posted deputies all over town. He figures that Nelson and Speck Webster might be coming in, and he gave orders to shoot them on sight. Don't want you to catch a stray slug, Lum," the voice said.

I crept to the front of the post office and peered through the window at the street. Two or three businesses were still open, including the general store from which the clerk was loading supplies into a wagon in front of his store.

Murky shadows filled the rest of the town, offering secluded hiding places from which the deputies could watch the main street.

"See anyone?" Lum whispered from behind me.

"Nope. Just shadows." I gestured to the wagon in front of the general store. "Whose wagon is that?"

The small man peered out the window. "That's Lester Potts. He ran the blacksmith shop. Lives on the edge of town out north. Hates Roche something fierce." He caught his breath. "Quick! Duck!"

I ducked into the shadows below the window just as two deputies walked past. After the sound of their footsteps faded, I peered over the windowsill and spotted two more men patrolling the far side of the street. I whistled softly. "They're thicker than horseflies in May."

"What are you going to do? You can't stay here all night."

"That wagon. If I can reach it without being spotted, I'll climb up on the undercarriage beneath the bed and ride it out of town right under the deputies' noses."

"That's easy. Go under the boardwalk out front."

I looked around at him. "Huh?"

He nodded. "Crawl under the boardwalk. It'll be muddy and wet, but the boardwalk is on piers like the buildings—a couple feet off the ground. You might have to squirm on your belly a piece, but you can crawl under the boardwalk right up to the wagon."

I considered his suggestion a moment. "I suppose that's the only choice I have. All right, now here's what I need you to do. I'll go out back and crawl under the boardwalk. Give me about ten minutes, then step out back and fire two shots into the air, one right after another. You hear?"

"Reckon so, but why?"

"A signal to Speck. When he hears your shots, he'll set off a stick of dynamite. That should give me enough of a distraction to scoot from under the board-walk to the wagon."

He hesitated. "What do I tell the sheriff when he asks what I was shooting at?"

I grinned. "Tell him you were shooting at me."

The ground beneath the boardwalk was cold, wet, and muddy, for which I was grateful. I had no doubt that in warm weather, the area beneath the boardwalk provided an ideal habitat for snakes, spiders, and cen-tipedes, all of which I avoided at all costs.

I crawled quickly, pausing each time I heard steps coming my way. Finally I reached the general store and squirmed to the edge of the boardwalk and waited.

A few seconds later, two shots rang out behind me followed twenty or thirty seconds later by a booming explosion back to the south.

Shouts and exclamations rang out, and running foot-steps pounded over my head. I waited a few moments, then hastily crawled from under the boardwalk and wedged myself between the bed and the undercarriage that linked the front and rear axles.

I had no sooner situated myself than a voice not five feet away startled me. "What do you figure that explo-sion was, Finas?"

"Beats me," another voice chuckled. "Might be that Nelson jasper tossing dynamite around again, Lester."

Lester laughed. "Not likely," he replied, climbing up on the spring seat of the farm wagon. "Thanks for the help loading, Finas."

"Anytime, Lester. You take care."

Lester Potts laid the reins across the rumps of his horses with a sharp pop. The wagon jerked forward. I lay on my back, my hands pressed against the bed, trying to maintain my balance as we bounced out of town.

A few minutes later, the wagon turned off the road and pulled around to the side of a small house and into a barn. No sooner had the driver reined up his team than he called, "All right, Mister Nelson. You can come out now."

I froze, then quickly shucked my Colt. Warily, I eased off the undercarriage and crawled from under the wagon. All I could see was the dark figure of a bulky hombre silhouetted against the dim light shining from a window in his house.

He turned. "Don't worry, I'm a friend. Come inside. Hurry. They're looking all over town for you."

Inside, Lester Potts hastily pulled the shades on his windows. He turned back to me, his gaze falling on the revolver in my hand. A crooked grin spread across his square face. He pulled off his battered hat and tossed it on the corner of a chair. "You won't need that," he said. "At least not in here. Anyone who's doing to Roche what you've been doing is a friend of mine."

Holstering my six-gun, I nodded. "Much obliged. I'm kind of surprised though since I burned your shop down."

He laughed. "You got no idea how that plumb tickled my funnybone. Roche owns the property, and he was claiming half of all I made. Now there ain't nothing to tax or get rent from. I'm moving out of here. Done sent my wife and young'uns to my brother's over in Homer."

I winced. "Hate to see you go. This could be a right pleasant little town."

"It was—" he hesitated, then added, "—before the war and before the carpetbaggers." He shook his head. "Shame it's in the shape it is now." He indicated the stove. "Want some coffee?"

His reply gave me an idea. "No, but maybe some information."

"Shoot."

"How many in town like you? I mean, fed up with Roche."

Lester scratched his thinning hair with his thick fingers. "Most, I reckon. When Roche come in a couple years back, we was all in sad condition. The war had plumb wore us down to skin and bones, and he come along and started buying up what he could. Folks had no choice but to sell out for pennies on the dollar or let the bank foreclose. That's how he got my shop." He paused and studied me a moment. "Why do you ask? You got some kind of plan?"

I looked him squarely in the eye. "I have a plan, but it's dangerous. And there is likely to be some killing," I added, my tone filled with foreboding.

Chapter Twenty-two

The blacksmith studied me several moments. He arched an eyebrow. "You talking about vigilantes—taking the law in your own hands?"

I nodded once and then waited for his response.

He chewed on his bottom lip. "Reckon I understand how you come up with that idea, but Roche has too many hired guns. Them of us here in town ain't gunnies. The only gun most of us has shot off is a Winchester .44 for deer or scattergun for birds."

"Could be that's all it would take if we all stuck together."

Lester pondered my response. "You reckon?"

"Last I heard, Roche had a dozen or so men left. We managed to scare a few out of town. If we can recruit

184

ten or fifteen who'll stand up with us, maybe we can whittle them down to size."

A frown wrinkled his broad forehead. "I don't know about that. Most of us, me among them, don't have the gumption to go face-to-face with Roche's hired guns."

I gave him a crooked grin. "Who said anything about face-to-face?"

The burly blacksmith frowned, then a faint grin spread over his face. "I believe I like the way you think, Mister Nelson."

"Make it Davy."

"Go on, Davy."

"How long would it take you to round up ten or fifteen men we can trust?"

"To go up against Roche?"

"Yes."

He shrugged. "Hard to say. Problem is that if they go up against Roche, and things go bad, they'll have to leave town."

"I know I'm asking a lot, but they have a lot at stake. They're going to have to decide if they want to keep living like they are, or if they want to live like free men."

Lester grimaced as he considered my words. Taking a deep breath and releasing slowly, he replied, "I'll do the best I can, but I ain't promising nothing."

I nodded. "That's all I ask. Now, we don't want to draw any attention, so whoever you get, have them drift out of town in different directions. We'll meet on top of the hill south of Otsie Bets' shack just before sundown day after tomorrow. There's a thick stand of pines on the hill. We can see for miles in every direction. Think you can manage that?"

"I can sure try."

I extended my hand. He took it and we shook. "Do your best. I've got a few things to check on between now and then. You just get me some men who want their town back."

We laid low the next day or so, although we did scout the Bar M from a distance. There was no activity in the place other than three horses in the corral.

Around noon on the second day, we headed for Otsie Bets' shack, each of us well aware that someone could have tipped Roche off and each aware that the more tracks we left in the mud and snow, the more likely Johnny Two-Shoes would cut our sign.

"We'll circle around and come in from the south. Keep your eyes moving. If Roche's hired hands are waiting for us, we'd blasted well better spot them first."

Mid-afternoon, we reined up in the middle of a stand of pine on a hill a mile or so from where we were to meet Lester Potts and his recruits. We dismounted and squatted in the shade to watch and wait. I rolled a cigarette and tossed the bag to Speck.

We smoked silently, our eyes scanning the rolling countryside sweeping away from us.

"Take a look," he whispered, nodding to the east.

Two riders had topped a hill and were trotting their ponies towards Bets' shack. "Roche's or Lester's?" Speck muttered.

I squinted at the two riders, trying to discern their features. "They don't ride like gun hands."

Over the next two hours, seven or eight more came in from every direction, all bearing down on the hill south of Bets' shack. I rose to my feet and flipped my cigarette to the ground and crushed it with the heel of my boot. I slipped the loop from the hammer of my Colt and slid the .44 up and down in my holster a few times. "Reckon it's time."

Speck drawled, "You reckon?"

"Yep."

The lanky cowpoke swung into his saddle. "You know we could be making a big mistake riding in there."

I climbed on my bay. I stared at him grimly. "I know."

Lester Potts nodded as Speck and I rode up through the pines. "Howdy, Nelson."

I nodded. "Lester." I eyed the others, eight altogether, fewer than I hoped, but perhaps enough to get the job done.

The thick-shouldered blacksmith gestured to the jasper at his side. "This here is Hank Warner. Hank runs the livery." Lester continued, introducing each of them to me and Speck. When he finished, I touched my forefinger to the brim of my Stetson. "Howdy, men."

They returned my greeting, their faces somber and their eyes reflecting their trepidation. I didn't blame them. I cleared my throat. "I figure since you're here, you'd like to send Carl Roche packing."

Several nodding heads confirmed my remark.

"Now, as long as he can keep hiring gunnies, the situation in Crockett won't change, so what we have to do is make sure word gets out that your town is mighty unhealthy on gunfighters."

One of the men spoke up, his voice filled with resignation. "But, what can we do? We sure can't ride into town and start shooting."

"You're right about that, Partner. We can't whip them on their home ground. We've got to draw them onto our territory. We've got to choose the time and place."

Lester frowned. "Our territory? What are you talking about, Nelson?"

"You men know those ridges north of town?"

"Yeah," one replied. "Five or six of them about a hundred feet high."

A slow grin curled my lips. "That's our territory."

"Huh?" My remark puzzled them.

"Tomorrow, meet Speck out there after your noon dinner. He'll place you on the slopes of the ridges overlooking the valley below. We'll catch them in a crossfire."

"How can you be sure they'll show up?" Lester asked.

"At two o'clock, I'm going to ride into town and shoot up the saloon and bank. Cooter and his boys will have to chase me."

A light of understanding filled Lester's eyes. "You're going to lead them right to us."

I nodded.

Two or three of the men exchanged worried looks. One, Hank Warner, spoke up. "Some of us ain't never killed nobody, Mister Nelson. Speaking for myself, I don't know that I could, even if it means getting our town back."

I understood exactly what he was saying. I'd felt the same way when Russell McCall and me faced the Yanks for the first time back in '61. "I don't care as much for killing those hardcases as I do making them leery of every corner they turn. If a jasper gets too spooky, nine times out of ten he'll light a shuck out of town. Besides," I added with a grin, "considering what Lester told me about you boys' marksmanship, I figure if one of those owlhoots gets killed, it'll be because he's so scared, he runs into a tree."

They all laughed.

I winked at Lester. He nodded back, going along with my white lie.

* * *

That night after we had climbed into our bedrolls, Speck muttered, "I wish tomorrow was over."

"It will be. Twenty-four hours from now, we'll have a heap better idea about which direction Crockett is heading."

Next morning, a weather front rolled in, bringing with it crisp clear air that promised chillier temperatures for the coming night.

Not long before noon, Speck and me parted, him heading for the ridges and me for Crockett. The closer I drew to the small village, the more nervous I became. I could feel my heart thudding against my chest. My lips were unnaturally dry.

There was still time to back out. I was taking a mighty risky chance. My pony could stumble. A lucky slug could catch me. They might give up pursuit before we reached the ridges. A hundred things that could go wrong tumbled about in my head.

And then I thought of Kate and the boys, wondering how they were and thinking how good it would be to see them. With them on my mind, some of my nervousness abated.

I pulled into a thicket of laurel south of town where I had a view of the main street. The street showed little activity. Was that because several of the men were out of town at the ridges or because of the nippy weather?

I pulled my watch from my vest pocket: 1:45.

Fifteen minutes to go. My bay must have sensed my apprehension for he jittered about nervously. "Easy, boy, easy," I whispered, leaning forward and patting his neck.

The next few minutes dragged. Finally, the minute hand touched twelve. I slipped my Winchester .44 from its boot and with a click of my tongue, sent my pony into a trot down the middle of the main street.

Too late to back out now, Davy, I told myself, levering a cartridge in the chamber. A few of the locals on the street eyed me curiously, but went about their business. I kept expecting a challenge, a shout, but none came.

Up the street on my left, the door to the tonsorial parlor opened, and a gent stepped out. Pulling his coat around himself tightly, he hurried up the boardwalk, paying me no attention.

Several horses were tied at the hitching rail in front of Roche's Saloon. I figured on tossing four or five slugs into the saloon, keeping them high so as not to accidentally hit anybody, then toss off a couple more down at the bank. And, I told myself, glancing at the sheriff's office across the street from the bank, I might as well give Cooter Fain a little surprise as well.

Just as I grew even with the saloon, Joe Beckner, his arm still in a sling, and another of Roche's men pushed through the batwing doors. They jerked to a halt, frozen in mid-step, staring at me in disbelief.

I threw the Winchester to my shoulder and pumped

five slugs into the saloon, sending the two hardcases diving back into the darkness of the saloon. I twisted around in my saddle and snapped off four slugs into the sheriff's office. "Let's go, Boy," I shouted, digging my spurs into my bay. As I sped past the bank, I loosed four more shots.

Behind me the town was in an uproar. Shots were discharged. Men shouted, and in the middle of the tumultuous clamor came the thunder of hoofbeats.

Booting the Winchester .30–30, I leaned forward and squeezed my legs hard against my horse's ribs, urging him into an all–out gallop. The trees lining the road flew by. Mud from my bay's hooves sprayed my legs.

I glanced over my shoulder. Five riders were after me. I grimaced. I'd hoped for more. Where were the others? Or had the postmaster, Lum Bishop, unintentionally provided me with an inaccurate number of Roche's gunmen?

My pursuers were about fifty or so yards behind, too far to hit anything except the ground with a handgun while bouncing in a saddle.

My heart leaped into my throat once when my horse stumbled, but he quickly caught himself.

Ahead, I spotted the ridges. Twisting in the saddle, I tossed off a shot at the riders behind, a signal to Speck and the men we were coming.

I planned on leading the unsuspecting pursuers between the two ridges on which Speck had stationed the men. We had men at either end and on the sides of the ridges. A neat trap. Still, I couldn't help wondering about the remainder of Roche's men. The discrepancy in numbers nagged at me.

Ahead, I spotted the ridges. I reined my bay between them and shot past a tangle of briars. I glanced back to see the riders enter the narrow valley between the ridges. Another few seconds.

Suddenly, gunfire erupted from above. I looked back, but the five riders had not slowed, had not reacted to the gunfire, but were continuing after me in a hard gallop.

A terrified shout rolled down the slopes of the ridges. I recognized the voice as Hank Warner's, the liveryman. "It's a trap. Roche's men have us trapped."

I shot a look up the slope and spotted three of our men running and stumbling down the slope. Above, on the crest of the ridge, stood Cooter Fain and two of his boys blasting away at the running men.

I couldn't believe my eyes. Carl Roche had turned our trap into one of his own, and was now eradicating his opposition.

Suddenly, a powerful blow struck my head. The last thing I remember is the ground coming up to meet me as I tumbled from my galloping pony.

Chapter Twenty-three

I awakened in the same jail cell in which I had spent my first night in Crockett. My head pounded, and when I opened my eyes, I felt as if Lester Potts, the blacksmith, was using my skull for an anvil.

Slowly I turned my head and peered through the bars. The jail was empty. I closed my eyes and tried to still the pulsating throbs hammering in my skull, trying to sort through the confusing mixture of thoughts rolling about in my head.

Speck? Where was Speck? I tried to concentrate, but the effort was too much, and I slipped back into the painless depths of unconsciousness.

Rough hands shook me awake.

The pounding in my head was still present. The con-

194

fusion remained, but at least I could focus on the two faces behind Sheriff Fain. One belonged to Lum Bishop, the postmaster. From the way the second one's nose was flattened all over his face, I guessed he was Roche's hired killer, Broken-Nose Jack.

"There you are, Lum," Cooter growled. "I told you he was just fine. Reckon he'll live long enough to hang."

In a prudish tone that surprised me despite the hammering in my head, the diminutive postmaster replied. "Good. I hope he gets what he deserves."

Broken-Nose Jack stared at me with eyes as cold as black ice. A sneer twisted his lips, and then without a word, he turned and left the jail.

Lum shivered after Jack closed the door. "He don't look like someone you'd want to cross."

The sheriff grunted, "I reckon you could say that. Now, what's this official government business you wanted to see me about?" He gestured to the chair in front of his desk.

Lum slipped into the chair. "Well, Sheriff," he began in an unnaturally loud voice. "Before Sheriff Swain was shot, he sent a letter off to St. Louis." He handed Cooter a letter. "This here's the reply. I figured since you was sheriff now, it should come to you."

Cooter opened the letter and frowned. He turned it upside down. His frown deepened.

"You want me to read it for you, Sheriff?" Lum innocently asked.

Hesitating momentarily, Cooter handed Lum the letter. "Reckon you can. My eyes been acting up."

With a wry grin, the postmaster skimmed the letter. "Says that a federal marshal is coming. I guess because of the letter Sheriff Swain wrote."

"Federal marshal?" Cooter Fain's brows furrowed in concern. "What for, do you figure?"

The bald postmaster shrugged. "No idea. I reckon he'll tell you when he gets here."

"It say when?"

"Anytime, I expect." He glanced at me, then turned back to the sheriff and in an unnaturally thunderous voice, asked, "Did your men ever find Nelson's partner, Speck Webster?"

My ears perked up.

"Nope. He got away cleaner than a hound's tooth."

His tone remaining loud, Lum remarked, "Too bad about those three getting themselves shot dead."

In a sanctimonious tone, Cooter replied, "Yep, but that's what happens when you go against the law."

Lum pushed to his feet and ran his hand over his shiny head. "Suppose you're right, Cooter. Good thing we got a smart gent like yourself for sheriff. See you later."

As he turned to leave, Lum glanced at me. "How you feeling, Nelson?"

Despite the confusion in my head, from the conversation between the postmaster and the sheriff, I knew Lum Bishop had not revealed our friendship.

"Suppose I've felt worse, but I can't remember when." I moved a leg and felt the knife in my boot press against my ankle. That was my ace in the hole.

His back to Sheriff Fain, Lum winked at me and spoke over his shoulder. "By the way, Sheriff. With a federal marshal on the way, I'd make sure Nelson here gets a fair trial."

Cooter's face contorted in anger. His voice belligerent, he snapped, "What do you mean by that? Are you accusing me of something?"

Lum turned back to Cooter. "Of course not, Sheriff, of course not. Why, the whole town knows you always follow the law. You just need to make sure other folks do. You're too good a man to take the blame for what someone else does."

"Huh?" Now clearly confused, Cooter stared at the postmaster.

Lum Bishop lowered his voice. "Look, Cooter. You know as well as me that Nelson yonder is a sore spot for Mister Roche. Now, I know Mister Roche won't do nothing against the law, but some of his men might figure he'd take kindly if they took matters into their own hands. You see what I mean?"

Cooter's face lit with understanding. "Yeah, reckon I do, Lum. Much obliged for the advice."

After the postmaster left, I feigned sleep. Footsteps approached the cell, paused, then receded. Moments later, the door slammed shut.

I sat up abruptly, and cringed as my head seemed to explode. I clenched my teeth and closed my eyes tightly until the pain eased to the merciful blows of a mere sledgehammer.

Finally, I opened them and peered around the cell. Rising gingerly, I crossed the squeaking floor to the cell door. I shook the door. It was snug. I muttered a curse when I tested the bars of the cell. They were rock solid. I cursed even more when I inspected the bars in the window. Roundheaded bolts fastened the iron bars to the wall.

Frustrated, I headed back to my bunk, but paused when one of the planks in the puncheon floor squeaked. I looked down and stepped off the twelve-inch-wide board, then back on it. It squeaked again, and I spotted movement in the plank.

Quickly, I fished my hunting knife with the four-inch blade from my boot and knelt at the seam where the end of the plank butted up against another. I inserted the tip of the blade between the two boards and gently pried. The tip slipped out, tearing out a sliver of wood.

I grimaced and glanced anxiously over my shoulder. I tried prying the board up once again, but another sliver of wood ripped away from the board. "Blast!" I muttered.

While I doubted Cooter would notice the shards missing from the floor, I couldn't afford to take a chance. Then my eyes fell on the bunk. Quickly, I pulled it out from the wall. I grinned when I spotted a gap between two planks that hadn't been butted together tightly.

Working feverishly, I pried one end loose so I could slip my fingers under it and lift it. Moments later, the six-foot board popped loose with a sharp snap. I froze, my eyes on the door.

Nothing.

Hastily, I turned back to the second board, which proved even easier to pop loose.

I dropped to my knees and stuck my head in the opening. I wanted to shout. The jail rested on piers like the other buildings in town. There was enough room for me to squirm under the floor.

Quickly, I fit the boards back into place and scooted the bunk over them. No sooner had I slipped the knife back in my boot and lain back on the bunk than the door opened. I looked up.

The sheriff sneered. "Awake, huh?"

Feigning dizziness, I struggled to my feet and clung to the bars. The sunlight flooding through the window behind me struck the far wall, indicating late afternoon. "What about some grub?"

"Prisoners get one meal a day, and you slept through yours."

I shook my head. "At least a drink of water."

Cooter curled his thin lips in disgust and snorted. Still, he dipped a tin cup in a bucket and handed it to me. The water was flat, but at that moment, it tasted like the expensive champagne sold in fancy restaurants like the Palmer House in Chicago.

"Thanks." I hesitated, then nodded to the rear door. "How about the privy. I've been here over twenty-four hours."

He glared at me, irritated. Then, with a long sigh, shucked his six-gun and opened the cell. "One wrong step, Nelson, and there won't be no need for a judge."

"Don't worry, Sheriff. I'm not stupid."

Outside, the air was growing nippy as the sun dropped lower on the horizon. The brisk air helped clear some of the cobwebs in my head.

Cooter followed me to the privy and back. I was grateful for the chance to stretch my legs, to work out some of the stiffness, and to take a quick survey of the buildings around me so when I made my break I wouldn't waste any time.

Back inside, the heat from the potbellied stove was a welcome respite from the chill outside. I sat on my bunk and watched as the sheriff plopped down at his desk and pulled a bottle of Old Orchard whiskey from the bottom desk drawer and filled a glass.

I spotted my Mackinaw on a peg on the wall. Next to it was my gunbelt—about six feet from the front door, I noted. Lying down, I pulled my blanket up about my neck. The heat put out by the stove was more than enough to offset the cold air drifting up between the boards in the floor.

I closed my eyes but my mind was racing, trying to figure out my first move after I escaped. A smart jasper would leave town by the first road, but I had no choice. I had made a promise to Russell McCall, and if I didn't carry it out, it would haunt me every day for the rest of my life—if I was lucky enough to live through the mess I was in.

Unfortunately, I had learned the hard way that Roche was too strong and had too many spies. I couldn't whip him with force, so I had to find another answer.

Kate and the others at the Bar M were convinced Roche had Ed McCall murdered after the old man made the mortgage payment in late December of the previous year. They couldn't prove it, so why did I think I could? No one dared testify against Roche. He was merciless with anyone who bucked him.

Maybe now with the federal marshal coming there might be something we could do, but what?

Then I remembered the bill of sale Roche had produced for the stolen cattle. What was it he had said? Something about his secretary notarizing the bill of sale.

I racked my brain, and then George Millikin's admission that night in the parlor of the Bar M exploded in my head: "Roche sent Cooter and Beckner out after McCall left the notary. When they came back, Cooter told Roche that McCall was took care of."

My eyes popped open, and I stared at the ceiling in

disbelief. The notary! Could that be the key to toppling Carl Roche? I tried to suppress my excitement. I could be heading into another box canyon.

Easy, Davy, I told myself. Take it easy. Think through it. According to Millikin, Ed McCall was at the notary. The only reason for McCall to be at the notary's was to validate his mortgage payment. If that were the case, then there should be a record of the transaction in the notary's log.

I grinned to myself. So, now all I had to do was break out of jail, make my way to the bank without being seen, find the notary journal, and live long enough to show it to the federal marshal.

Simple.

I heard the sheriff's chair scrape on the floor and instantly closed my eyes. His footsteps came toward me and paused. I breathed slowly and regularly. After a few moments, the footsteps headed across the floor, pausing again at the desk. In the next second, the room fell dark. Moments later, the door slammed, and I breathed a sigh of relief.

Now for the hard part.

Chapter Twenty-four

Just in case the sheriff decided to return, I waited for what seemed like an hour before making my move. When I finally decided he was gone for the night, I rolled out of my blankets and slid the bunk away from the wall. I shaped the blankets to appear as if I were asleep after which I quickly removed the boards and eased to the ground underneath. I slid the bunk back in place over my head.

Water from the previous snow and icy drizzle had gathered under the jail. By the time I squirmed from under the clapboard building, I was shivering and covered with mud.

Remaining in the shadows, I sloshed my way through the mud to the front of the jail. For long seconds in the shadows cast by the corner of the jail, I studied the torch-lit street, all the while trying to still the chills wracking my thin frame. Taking a deep breath, I slid along the front of the jail and through the door where I grabbed my heavy coat and gunbelt.

Back outside in the shadows between the buildings, I strapped on my Colt and slipped into the Mackinaw, grateful for the warmth of the heavy coat.

Now, I told myself, I needed someplace to hide out until tomorrow, someplace no one would think of looking. That's when I remembered the top floor of the bank, the one of which the bookkeeper, Ezekiel Watts, and the general store clerk had spoken my first day in Crockett.

A crooked grin played over my lips. That would be the last place that Roche or the sheriff would think to look.

Although the torches lit the street dimly, I decided that rather than chance being seen crossing the street, I'd circle around town and come into the bank from the rear. I didn't encounter a soul. Once or twice when a dog barked, I'd pause and crouch in the shadows.

Finally, I reached the rear of the bank where I tested the windows. Locked!

Next I tried the side and discovered one window unlocked. Glancing around nervously, I eased it open. I swung a leg over the sill, then froze. I had been slogging through ankle-deep mud, and it clung to my boots in thick chunks. I couldn't take a chance of leaving tracks on the floor.

I scooted up until I sat astraddle the sill, slipped the boot off my right foot, and then stepped to the floor in my socks. I removed the other boot before stepping inside. After lowering the window, I paused, boots in hand while my eyes grew accustomed to the darkness.

Pale light from the sputtering street torches flickered across the floor. A railing and a teller's cage with wrought-iron bars reaching the ceiling bisected the room. Behind the railing, I made out three desks and behind them, a stairway leading to the second floor. Beneath the stairs was a door. I eased up the stairs. At the top, all before me was black, as if I'd closed my eyes. Extending my arm, I felt back and forth for a wall, but there was nothing but space. I eased forward, still in my stockings, still feeling ahead.

More space.

I took another step and touched a wall. For a moment, I stood staring into the complete darkness. I decided to do something smart for a change and stop blundering about so I sat and pulled on my boots and leaned back against the wall. "Might as well wait until it's light enough to see," I muttered.

During the night, the wind rose and the temperatures fell. I sat hunched over, trying to preserve as much heat as possible. The wind continued to blow, rattling the windowpanes below. Slowly, false dawn grayed the sky, and I could see my frosty breath in the frigid air.

I looked around. I was on a landing. Two doors opened to other rooms. I hesitated, checking my boots. The mud had dried. Gently moving across the landing, I opened the first door and peered into a storeroom where boxes of bank records were stacked next to a window. Quickly, I slipped behind the boxes and scraped the larger chunks of mud from my boots. Then I inspected the other room, which contained empty wooden crates and various pieces of furniture. In the center of the ceiling was a trap door.

Back on the landing, I discovered that there was no way I could observe those below from the landing without being seen myself. For a moment, I considered my predicament.

Hastily, I returned to the second room. I stacked crates until I could open the trap door. I peered inside.

Perfect. Climbing into the attic, I found a few loose planks, which I laid over the ceiling joists, after which I used my knife to punch a peephole in the pressed tin ceiling. I pressed my eye to it. I could see both the business area and the lobby of the bank below. The door under the stairs had an opaque glass window. I made out gold printing on the window. "Roche's office," I muttered, although I couldn't make out the words.

I studied the room below. "Not bad, Davy, not bad," I whispered to myself. "Now, just cross your fingers and pray for a little luck."

I lay back on the boards, my arms wrapped around

my chest, waiting for the bank to open. From the light streaming through the tiny hole, I could see my frosty breath.

Sometime later, the faint jingle of metal against metal caught my attention. Slowly, I rolled over and peered through the tiny hole. The door opened and Ezekiel Watts, the bookkeeper and notary public entered, his drab black coat buttoned tightly about his thin chest against the cold. He quickly closed the door and built a fire in the potbellied stove behind the banister, after which he disappeared into Roche's office.

When he returned, he went about getting the bank ready for business.

I shifted about, trying to relieve my cramped muscles.

The thin bookkeeper opened the vault and removed a stack of journals. Excitement coursed through my veins. Were those the ones I was looking for? And if they were, then what? Just how in the Sam Hill was I going to put my hands on them?

At that moment, the frail-looking bookkeeper answered the question for me.

Buttoning his coat, he put on his hat and left the bank, locking the door behind him. Hastily, I descended to the room below, taking time to replace the trapdoor. I made it to the stairs in time to see the thin man enter Rosie's Café next to the sheriff's office across the street.

"Talk about luck," I gushed, taking the stairs two at a time. I headed directly for the journals on the corner of his desk. The titles of each journal were written in fancy calligraphy on white labels. I shuffled through them, stopping when I found the title, *Notary Log*.

The front door rattled.

I dropped to a crouch and peered over the desk. My heart leaped into my throat. Carl Roche stood hunched over the lock on the door. The crisp click of falling tumblers broke the silence like gunshots.

Quickly, I scurried behind the half-wall separating the teller's cage from the office. The door slammed. I pressed up against the solid panels of the wall as foot-steps approached. To my relief, they passed and moments later, I heard Roche's door close.

I scooted around the half-wall, planning on exiting through the front door when I saw Ezekiel mounting the steps to the porch.

The only choice I had was to hide upstairs. On tip-toe, I mounted the stairs and darted into the room where the bank stored its records. I pressed up against the door, my heart thudding in my chest like an Indian drum.

I crossed the room and crouched behind the stack of records by the window. I ran the tip of my finger down the list of signatures and transactions in the journal for the month of December, 1866.

My breath caught in my throat when I found the entry. *December 29, 1866. Ed McCall*, $1,300. *Paid against Bar M loan, reducing the balance to $7,400.*

My hands shook with excitement.

I froze when I heard the sound of footsteps coming up the stairs. I slammed the log shut and crouched lower behind the boxes of records just as the door opened. I glanced to my right. I grimaced. If whoever opened the door took another step or two, he'd spot me.

Suddenly a voice from below echoed up the stairs. "Ezekiel!"

A voice just beyond the boxes replied, "Yes, Sir, Mister Roche."

"I want to see you, now!"

His voice trembling with anxiety, the bookkeeper replied, "Yes, Sir. Right away, Sir."

I breathed a sigh of relief when the door slammed shut. Quickly I rifled through the pages of the journal to the page with McCall's mortgage payment. I ripped it from the journal and folded it into my shirt pocket. "Now," I muttered, snapping the journal shut. "All I have to do is get this log back on the bookkeeper's desk."

Opening the door a crack, I peered onto the landing. Voices came up from below, and moments later I spotted the back of the diminutive bookkeeper scurrying out the front door. That still left Roche below.

Easing through the door, I tiptoed to the top of the stairs, notary log in hand. If I could make it to the bottom of the stairs, I could toss it on the floor beside the desk. With luck, the bookkeeper would just assume it had fallen.

I started down the stairs, but as I did I spotted

Sheriff Fain running across the street toward the bank. Hastily, I slipped back into the storeroom, leaving the door open a crack.

Fain burst into the bank and raced to the rear, shouting, "Mister Roche! Mister Roche!" He threw open the office door.

Roche exclaimed. "What—"

The sheriff cut him off. "Nelson's escaped, Mister Roche. Nelson's escaped."

"What?"

"He's gone. Sometime during the night."

Roche cursed. Their voices grew more distinct as they emerged from the banker's office. Roche screamed, "Where were you, you stupid fool?"

"At home. I locked him up tight before I left last night, Mister Roche. Honest."

"You should have stayed the night at the jail."

With a plaintive whine in his voice, Fain replied, "But I always sleep at home, Mister Roche."

"Why are you just now telling me? It's almost nine-thirty."

"Because I thought he was sleeping. He done bundled up the blankets to make it look like he was sleeping. When I went to wake him, I saw what he had done."

"How'd he escape?"

"Pulled up the floor under his bunk."

Roche cursed again. He grabbed his hat and strode purposefully toward the door. "Come on, you worthless—Go get Broken-Nose Jack. Time for him to earn his keep. And find Johnny Two-Shoes. Put him on to tracking Nelson." He sputtered, "Get your men out. Have them block off every road out of town." The slamming of the front door cut off his tirade.

Without hesitation, I raced down the stairs, placed the notary log back on the stack of journals, and headed for the back door. I grabbed the doorknob and froze as a stark question hit me between the eyes. How the Sam Hill did I figure on getting out of town? No horse, everyone in town looking for me, the streets blocked off . . .

My eyes traveled up the wall to the ceiling above. Why not? The storeroom where I'd previously hidden. No one would think of looking there, and if they did, I still had the window. If I could stay out of sight until nighttime, then I'd slip out the window, drop to the ground, and vanish like a ghost into the woods behind the bank.

Chapter Twenty-five

The day passed slowly. By noon, the hubbub stirred up by my escape had slackened somewhat, but from my window, I could see Roche's men still patrolling the streets.

All I had to do until the federal marshal arrived was stay out of Roche's hands. Simple logic, but much more difficult to carry out in practice.

My mouth was drier that the West Texas desert, and I couldn't remember the last meal I'd put myself around. My stomach growled like a mama grizzly protecting her cubs. I cinched up my belt a couple notches, a Spanish supper.

Throughout the day, the clouds thickened, a portent of rain or snow. The temperatures dropped. Early afternoon, the bookkeeper stopped feeding the fire, and by the time he locked the door behind him, the storeroom was twenty degrees colder.

Because of the cloud cover, night came early.

Dusk settled over the small town at the same time the snow began. I slipped downstairs, pausing at the hat rack to grab a sombrero and tug it down over my head.

Slowly, I opened the back door, peered up and down the alley, then slipped outside into the falling snow. I hurried past Wells Fargo to the post office. I knocked softly on Lum Bishop's back door.

The door opened slightly, and Lum peered out. When he saw me, he jerked the door open. "Davy! Get in here. Quick. The whole town's looking for you." He shut the door and pulled the shades on the windows.

"Where the blazes you been all day?"

I nodded to the coffee on the stove. "I could sure use some of that coffee. I got mighty thirsty up in the storeroom over Roche's office."

He looked around at me in surprise and then a big grin spread over his weathered face. "Well, I swan. You was up over Roche's head all day while he was out beating the bushes for you? That's a rib-tickler." He shook his head. "Help yourself, Davy. Don't reckon you've had nothing to eat neither."

I patted my stomach. "Not for the last two days."

"Well, you sit. I'll fry us up some steak and heat up the leftover beans."

While I shoveled his grub down my gullet, I told

him about the entry in the notary log and my intentions of giving it to the federal marshal.

"If Roche lets you live that long," the older man replied ominously.

"He's got to catch me first, and I sure won't make the same mistake as before. Any idea about Speck?" I sipped my coffee.

"Nope." He chewed on his lip. "I figure he's laying mighty low, waiting to see what's going to happen around here."

"What about the others? You said three of them were killed in the ambush?"

He nodded slowly.

"What about Lester Potts?"

His face softened in relief. "No. He got away. Got no idea where he is, but he got away. Probably went on to Homer to join up with his family." He studied me a few moments. "What're you going to do next?"

I shrugged. "Stay out of sight until the marshal arrives. That's all I know to do."

Nodding slowly, Lum said, "I'll see about getting you a horse tomorrow."

"Maybe I should try to get out of town tonight. We can meet somewhere."

"Where do you have in mind?"

"Just head into the woods behind the post office. I'll be out there somewhere."

"Good."

Before I left, Lum rolled me up some grub in a couple blankets and a canvas tarp. "You'll need this out there tonight," he muttered, nodding to the door. Then he blew out the lantern. "Wait a few minutes before you slip out. If anyone's out there, they'll figure I'm done gone to bed."

I looked in the direction of his voice. "Roche and his men been watching you?"

"They're watching everybody."

I cursed under my breath, now more determined than ever to see this through to the end.

Sometime later, I slipped out the back door and hurried to the stand of pines some thirty yards behind the post office. Once inside the pines away from the peripheral light cast by flickering torches along the street, I had to feel my way. Several times, I stumbled over dead limbs, through tangles of briars, and when I climbed over a fallen pine, I decided to curl up beside it, using the thick trunk to break the chilling wind.

As I squirmed down into my cocoon of blankets and canvas, I thought I heard shouts above the rushing of wind through the treetops. I paused and lifted my head, straining my ears, but all I heard was the wind weaving its winter song through the treetops.

When I peeked out from under the tarp next morning, the ground was covered with snow. The sky through the treetops was brittle blue, and the air was crisp and sweet, the kind of morning made for steam-

ing six-shooter coffee and hot saddle blankets smoth-
ered with molasses.

All I had was cold biscuits and cold steak, but
compared to other times when I had to settle for nothing more than Spanish suppers, this breakfast was
delicious.

Later, I found a spot within the pines where I could
watch the post office. I didn't want to miss Lum when
he brought my horse. I figured once I was on horse-
back, I'd make myself scarcer than whiskey at a
Baptist Bible class until the marshal arrived. I might
even get lucky enough to hook up with Speck.

The day passed slowly, and with each hour, my
patience grew thinner. What was taking the old man so
long?

From time to time, Roche's men rode along the rear
of the buildings, studying the pines. Each time, I eased
behind a tree trunk even though I knew their eyes
could not penetrate back into the shadows where I
crouched.

Mid-afternoon, half a dozen riders gathered behind
the post office. Cooter Fain was giving instructions
and pointing in my direction. Then he gestured for
them to spread out.

My blood ran cold.

I didn't know what had happened, but it looked
mighty certain to me those jaspers were heading my
way. Had Lum Bishop given me away?

There was no time to wonder. I scurried back into the woods, trying to travel in those spots where the trees had blocked the snow from the ground.

Behind me, horses whinnied, and men cursed, but they continued moving into the woods, driving me deeper and deeper. Ahead, I spied a snow-covered hump that turned out to be a dead tree covered with vines. If I crawled under the vines and hunkered up against the tree trunk, perhaps they wouldn't spot my tracks.

I glanced over my shoulder. I couldn't see the riders but I could hear them. Hastily, I backed into the windfall, trying to smooth my tracks in the snow. Finally, I was inside. Above was a thin canopy of snow over the vines.

The sounds of the posse grew more distinct. I unleathered my six-gun, a futile gesture considering I was up against six gunnies, but I felt better with the Colt clutched in my hand.

By now, the sounds of the trackers were all around me. Voices called back and forth, each edged with exasperation and frustration.

"I don't see no sign of Nelson, Cooter."

Another shouted. I recognized the voice as belonging to Joe Beckner. "If that old man lied to us, I'll give him another whipping he won't forget."

I grimaced. Anger surged in my veins, roared in my ears. I wanted to burst out of the windfall with my Colt blazing, but I knew that was a fool's play. I lay motionless and waited, hoping the old postmaster hadn't taken too much of a beating at the hands of Cooter Fain and Roche's gunhands.

Finally, the sounds faded away, but I still didn't emerge from my snug refuge.

As dusk approached, I slipped out and made my way back toward the town. I crouched behind a fallen log several feet inside the timberline.

The sky was clear and much of the snow remained. The starlight reflecting off the snow would provide enough of a background for me to travel through the edge of the forest.

I planned to circle town, wait until early morning, then slip into the livery and find me a horse. Once I was away from town, I'd find me a snug hideout and wait for the marshal. With a smug grin, I patted my shirt pocket where I had folded the page from the notary log.

Despite my predicament, I felt fairly confident that Carl Roche's days were numbered, and that number corresponded to the days until the federal marshal arrived.

I should have known better than to be so cocksure of myself.

As shadows began to settle over the small village, a handful of Roche's men carrying lanterns came from between the Wells Fargo office and the post office. Instantly, every one of my senses grew alert. I readied myself to disappear back into the woods, but instead of heading in my direction, they stopped in front of Lum Bishop's back door. One stepped forward, holding his lantern high. "Nelson. This is Sheriff Fain," he shouted. "If you're out there, I got a surprise for you. A friend of yours here wants to see you."

He gestured to the cluster behind him, and suddenly a small figure stumbled into the lantern light.

It was ten-year-old Sam McCall.

Chapter Twenty-six

My blood ran cold. How the Sam Hill did they get the boy?

The sheriff called out again. "We got the whole bunch, Nelson. They're accused of killing John Bratton out at the Bar M. Ambushed him while he was doing his duty as a deputy."

I cursed.

"You got a choice, Nelson. Let them take the blame, or you come in and take it."

Some choice. I had just been dealt a loser's hand, but more than once, I had seen a bad hand turn out a winner if a jasper just remained calm.

Unbuttoning my Mackinaw, I slipped the evidence against Roche from my pocket and pulled open a thread on my vest and inserted the folded document in the lining where I once stashed what few greenbacks I had. I pulled the thread back through the hole and knotted it.

"Nelson! You hear me?"

Taking a deep breath, I rose slowly. "I hear you. I'm coming out. Don't shoot." I hoped Cooter Fain remembered the warning Lum Bishop had given him a few days earlier.

I stepped from the trees, hands over my head.

Half a dozen guns lined up on me. "Keep your hands up," shouted Cooter. "Walk over here. Joe, get his gun."

With a leer, Joe Beckner circled behind me and relieved me of my Colt. The next second, thousands of stars exploded in my head.

I slowly became aware of a damp rag bathing my face. I opened my eyes and looked up into Kate's. Her brows knit with worry, she whispered, "How are you feeling?"

"I'll live," I muttered. "How—how did you get here?"

Her voice grew bitter. "Roche's men. They found us in Sumter and dragged us back. Smoke tried to stop them, but they hurt him bad. I think they broke one of his arms."

I grimaced and closed my eyes against the throbbing in the back of my head. "The boys—are they hurt?"

"No."

The door to the cell squeaked open. Cooter Fain stepped into the lantern light. "That's it, Miss McCall. Time's up."

"But—"

"Sorry. Prisoner gets no more visitors. He's got to have his rest for the trial in the morning." Keeping his eyes on her, he said. "Joe, you and one of the boys take Miss McCall and the boys over to the hotel. Mister Roche has rooms for them. And make sure they don't leave, you hear?"

Beckner grunted, "Don't worry. They won't."

I tried to swing my legs off the bunk to the floor, but my left leg was jerked to an abrupt halt after only a few inches.

Cooter laughed. "You ain't escaping this time, Nelson. I chained you to the bunk. And I'm leaving two deputies here tonight to watch you. I want you around for the trial and hanging in the morning."

I still had my knife in my boot, but a knife was no good against a chain, and with two of Roche's gun-hands watching me, I couldn't hack through the heavy post around which I was shackled.

Throughout the long night, I tried to engage the two in conversation, perhaps create an opportunity, however slight, to escape; but they refused to say a word. They sat in chairs with Winchesters across their laps, glaring at me.

*   *   *

Morning came all too soon.

At nine o'clock, Cooter and four other gunnies came into the cell. Without warning, they grabbed me and rolled me over on my belly, tying my hands behind my back. Then Cooter unshackled me from the bunk and rough hands jerked me to my feet. "Joe, you grab hold of the end of chain so he can't run. Okay, boys, get him over to the saloon."

As I stepped out on the boardwalk, I looked around. At the south end of the main street, several horsemen sat under a spreading oak from which dangled a rope.

I glanced up at the hotel and saw Kate staring at me wide-eyed, her face drawn with anguish. I wished I had thought to tell her about the evidence in my vest. Even if Roche hanged me, she could still have beaten him. As it was now, the evidence that would have convicted Carl Roche was going to the grave with me.

Unless—I wondered if I could wrangle a last-minute conversation with Lum Bishop. I could pass word to him, and he could get it to Kate.

Chapter Twenty-seven

Outside the saloon, Joe Beckner removed the chain from my ankle. The sheriff held the door open and shoved me inside.

The saloon had been rearranged into a courtroom. A poker table served as the judge's bench. On either side sat an empty chair in front of which were four or five rows of chairs filled with local citizens as well as some of Roche's gunnies.

Leaning back on his elbows, Broken-Nose Jack slumped lazily against the bar, a sneer twisting his thin lips. The first time I'd laid eyes on the killer, an aura of evil had seemed to surround him. That same feeling now filled the saloon.

I shouldn't have been surprised, but I was when I saw Carl Roche with a smug grin on his fleshy face, sitting behind the poker table that served for a judge's bench. Strange what a jasper notices at times like this. I had once noted the wart on his bulbous nose, and now I spotted a black hair growing out of the wart.

The sheriff untied my hands and shoved me into a chair on one side of the bench. I looked over the gallery. I stiffened in shock when I saw Lum Bishop, his face bruised, his eyes black and swollen. He was staring at the floor.

Flexing my fingers into claws, I glared at Cooter Fain. He sneered and grinned.

Carl Roche called court to order. There were no preliminaries, no opening statements. He called the first witness, Joe Beckner.

The bailiff, one of Roche's hardcases, swore Beckner in.

Roche cleared his throat, ready to hammer the last nail in my coffin. "Tell us what you know about the murder of John Bratton at the Bar M, Joe—I mean, Mister Beckner."

Favoring his broken arm, Beckner cleared his throat. "Well, Bratton and me was playing poker when Nelson yonder busted through the door and shot poor old Bratton deader than a beaver hat. Gave him no chance at all. He woulda shot me too, but I jumped out a window and got away." He paused, grinning at me smugly.

"Anyone with him?"

"Huh? Well, there was George Millikin. Nelson was holding a gun on him."

"And where is Millikin now?"

Beckner shrugged. "I don't know, Mister Roche—I mean, Judge. I ain't seen him since that night. Likely Nelson or Speck killed him too."

Roche lifted an eyebrow. "Speck?"

"Yes, sir. Speck Webster. He was right in the thick of it with Nelson there."

At that moment, I wouldn't have given a plugged nickel for my chances.

Judge Roche grinned wickedly. "Speck Webster, huh? Any idea where that gent is?"

The batwing doors of the saloon swung open, and a voice responded to his question. "I'm right here, Judge."

The entire room turned to see Speck Webster standing in the open door with a drawn six-gun, a tall, steely-eyed stranger at his side.

Roche barked, "Sheriff, arrest that man."

Broken-Nose Jack grabbed for his six-guns with both hands, but froze when the stranger's voice boomed. "Hold it right there, Sheriff. Nobody is arresting anyone unless I say so."

His voice rising in fury, Roche demanded, "Who do you think you are, disturbing the sanctity of this court?"

The stranger took a step forward and pulled back

the lapel of his heavy sheep-lined coat. "Name's Hank Farrell, Federal Marshal out of St. Louis, Missouri." The room grew silent as he looked around. "The reason I'm here is that the agency got a letter from Sheriff Swain, who, according to Mister Webster here, was shot and killed. The sheriff inquired about a gent named Carl Roche."

My hopes soared.

Roche's eyes widened in surprise. "That's me. Why would he be writing about me?"

Farrell shrugged. My elation crumbled when the marshal replied, "Can't say. You ain't wanted for nothing, but my supervisor recognized your name and asked me to get a deposition from you about an incident you witnessed up in St. Louis before you came down here."

A smile of relief relaxed the tense features in Roche's face, but instantly grew taut again as the marshal continued. "But Mister Webster here has been telling me a few things about this town that my supervisor might think needs looking into."

Everyone was staring at the marshal, ignoring me. I stood up. "How about murder, Marshal?"

Every eye turned back to me. I pointed to Carl Roche. I have proof this man murdered Ed McCall in December of last year."

The saloon erupted with shouts of anger and surprise.

Cooter Fain cursed and started toward me, but the boom of a six-gun halted him in his tracks. "Nobody move," Marshal Farrell shouted, smoke drifting up from the muzzle of his big Walker Colt. "Now sit, every last one of you hombres. Squat."

They squatted.

He looked at me. "Your name Davy Nelson?"

"Yes." I fished the page of the notary log from the lining of my vest and held it up. "There isn't a soul in this room who hasn't heard Carl Roche swear that Ed McCall gambled his mortgage payment away in the saloon that night."

Several heads nodded in agreement. I continued, "And Mister Roche has admitted he wants the Bar M."

Roche looked at the paper in my hand, a frown on his sweaty forehead. His face blanched when I said, "This is a page on which his Notary Public, Ezekiel Watts, swore that on December 29, 1866, Ed McCall paid one thousand, three hundred dollars to Carl Roche for the annual payment on his ranch—a payment Roche claimed he never received."

Roche's eyes grew wide, and he looked around frantically. "That's a lie," he shouted. "He forged the signature."

The marshal strode across the room toward me. "Let me see that." He held out his hand.

"Here. And if you'll go to the notary log at the bank, you'll see the torn edges match those in the log." From the corner of my eye, I saw Roche jerk his head around in the direction of the bar.

In the next second, Broken-Nose Jack's six-guns

jumped into his hand as if by magic. "Marshal! Look out," I shouted.

He spun too late.

With two ear-splitting explosions, Jack's Colts belched orange plumes of fire and smoke. One slug caught Marshal Farrell, knocking him back into me. The second missed him, smashing a leg on the chair in which I had been sitting.

I didn't hear the shouts of terror or the screams of fear. All I could focus on was the big .45 Walker Colt spinning from the marshal's hand. I grabbed at it with both hands as his bulk knocked me backward.

As I tumbled back over my chair, I kept my eyes on the Colt, my fingers desperately trying to seize it. My shoulder hit the floor, and my head cracked against the wooden planks, but by now, I held the Colt firmly with both hands around the frame.

As I rolled over onto my belly, I shifted the six-gun to my right hand and hauled back on the hammer. Chunks of the floor exploded in front of me. I swung the muzzle of my Colt around and laid the front sight in the middle of Broken-Nose Jack's chest as the gunman crouched in front of the bar, his rotting teeth bared in a snarl, both handguns roaring.

Suddenly, a powerful blow struck my bad leg. I grimaced, but squeezed off a shot. I thumbed back the hammer, and fired again, and again.

Smoke thickened in the room, and I could no longer see Broken-Nose Jack.

I paused, the Walker Colt cocked, and waited, peering into the haze filling the saloon.

After the clamor of gunfire, the silence that spread over the saloon was deafening.

I blinked several times, trying to see Jack before he spotted me, and then I saw him, sprawled on the floor in front of the bar.

Speck knelt at my side. "Davy! You hurt?"

"No. I don't think so. Here. Help me up."

He helped me to my feet, and I promptly collapsed, a searing pain ripping through my gimpy leg.

"You've been shot," he shouted.

He was right. The thigh of my denims was soaked with blood.

"I'll get the doc."

"Wait." I scanned the saloon, which was slowly coming back to life. "Where's Roche?"

Speck cursed. "He ain't here. He musta took off."

"Forget about me then. Get out there and try to stop him."

The lanky cowpoke bolted for the door, but before he reached it, the batwings swung open. Carl Roche, followed by Cooter Fain and five of Roche's hired guns marched in, hands over their heads. Behind them came Lester Potts and half a dozen citizens, each carrying a double-barreled scattergun.

Chapter Twenty-eight

Next morning with Kate driving and the boys in the back of the buckboard, we headed back to the Bar M. Speck rode alongside.

The sky was clear and the air was clean. "Seems like a brand-new world," Kate said, glancing at me.

"Reckon it is, with Roche in jail and Marshal Farrell in charge. I imagine it won't take long for Crockett to turn itself into a nice little town where a man won't mind settling his family."

"Sure was a fine sight to see Lester Potts and his boys holding them scatterguns on Roche," Speck drawled. "Never figured they had the sand to do it."

I shrugged. "Can't tell about folks, Speck. Sometimes they do what you least expect."

Sam McCall piped up. "You gonna stay with us at

the Bar M, Davy? We sure need a foreman bad. Kate says she hopes you do."

"Sam! You hush up, you hear," Kate snapped, her face crimson. "Besides, Davy's headed for California."

Ray McCall, a frown on his face, asked, "You still going to California, Davy?" His tone was pleading.

For the first time since I was a younker, I had a feeling that I had found a place I could call home. "Well, Ray, California is a place I wanted to go."

"But why?"

I sensed Kate was watching from the corner of her eyes. "No particular reason. It was there, and I'm here."

"But the Bar M is here, and you're here. Seems like it'd save a heap of traveling," the young man replied.

Speck spoke up. "That boy makes about the best sense I've heard in a long time, if you ask me, not that you did," he added hastily

"Well," I drawled, looking around at Kate. "I reckon it depends on the boss and if she needs a foreman, one who'd figure on staying around for a good spell."

She looked up at me, a smile as wide as the Trinity River on her lips. "Only way is if the new foreman agrees to stay on for the next fifty years."

I leaned forward and touched my lips to hers. "I reckon he does."